WHOSE WIFE IS SHE?

Reverse Harem BWWM Mafia Romance

Jolie Damman

ISBN: 9798808556263
Imprint: Independently published

1st edition

Cover design by: Jolie Damman

CONTENTS

CHAPTER 1

Ferlisha

I woke up and everything around me was dark. I started to panic, mostly because the first thought that came to my mind was that I was going blind. But then I realized that it wasn't the case. I could see at least a fraction of what was around me. So much so that I was already calming down, even though my heart was still speeding up.

I was on a bed, and I sat up on it. Turning my head from left to right, I couldn't even figure out where I was. It appeared to be a bedroom, but even that wasn't clear to me. I was thinking that because the room where I was had bookcases and a couple of other things that told me it was probably also used for something else.

I reached out with my hand to the nightstand that was by my side and pulled the little cord that belonged to a table lamp. When I did that, a ball of light immediately illuminated the room, making me blink twice as I tried to understand and figure out where I was.

I didn't remember being in this house, even though I was partying pretty hard and so many things could've happened after I started to drink too much.

I should have heeded my brother's warnings. He said that I shouldn't drink too much, but I just brushed him off.

My eyes went down as I panicked again. I did remember that

I was partying, but I couldn't remember anything about the wedding dress that I was wearing. Unless it was for some kind of Halloween party, it didn't make any sense that I wore this wedding dress for it.

I couldn't have been in a marriage, right? It couldn't have been my marriage.

I slid off the bed and proceeded out of the room. I wasn't going to find anything in there, anyway. Not to mention that the first thing I needed to do now was to get out of this house, wherever it was.

I remembered that I was partying, that it was great, that I was having a good time, but then I also remembered that there was nothing else after that in my mind. Nothing that I could even try to bring up.

I proceeded out of the room and found myself in a dark, foreboding hallway where it felt like the air around me was heavier than normal. I felt like my heart was going to burst and that I was going to start crying. I tipped up my chin and decided that I wasn't going to let either of those things happen.

Even though the hallway was dark and I couldn't see any light switches anywhere, I wasn't going to show weakness. I wasn't going to show that I was afraid. I was done doing any of those things.

I started down the hallway and reached what appeared to be the area of the second floor that led to the main hall. I glanced around me as I realized that this 'house' was more like a mansion. It was big, massive, and mostly made of wood. Even the staircase in front of me was made of wood.

It was a dark, high-quality type of wood, I noticed. I could move my hand over it and feel the quality of it, but I didn't. I just didn't want to feel how cold it probably was. I knew it was cold even though the air around me felt normal, mostly because I noticed the snow outside. It was everywhere and painting the landscape in white, and I couldn't see much of it.

It was so dark outside and I could hear the wind howling. It wasn't just enough that it was snowing, but it also needed to be a bloody snowstorm, I thought as I began to panic once again.

It seemed that I was in a mansion somewhere in a forest, where most likely not even phone signal reached this place.

With that thought in mind, my hand started to look for a pocket in the wedding dress, but I found none. I was a little disappointed, but it was expected. I figured that the wedding dress didn't have a pocket before I even tried to find one.

The good thing was that I still remembered most of what happened previously, before that party, but it was still a little fuzzy to me. The only thing I could remember was my name. Ferlisha. It was a beautiful, special name that I liked. I was happy with it and I never thought about changing it.

Given that there was nothing else to do here, I decided to walk down the staircase to the first floor. I was going to try opening the door and, if I was in luck, when I was outside, I would find someone.

I wouldn't be able to stay outside for long mostly because of the cold and the snow. Given how much it was snowing and how strong the wind was, I couldn't stay out in the open for long.

I reached the first floor and started to make my way toward the main door as I thought I heard a noise coming from one of the other rooms. For a moment, I thought that it was just the wind that did that, but then I started to think what if there was someone else in the mansion?

It was possible, given how massive it was. It would take me more than a couple of minutes to fully explore the place and, even then, I would still think that there were probably some hidden rooms scattered throughout it.

Maybe even a basement, though I shuddered just thinking about it. The reason why I felt that way was because I used to play Resident Evil when I was little and one of the things I most remembered about it was what was hidden in the basement in that game.

I never thought I would find myself in a similar mansion in my life. I always thought that it was something that only happened in my dreams.

I stopped behind the door, tried the doorknob, and when I realized that it wasn't turning, I wasn't surprised. I was panicking a little, but I wasn't surprised.

What surprised me was finding out that my finger had a marriage ring on it. I was beginning to think that I was really getting married before this happened, even though I couldn't even remember the slightest thing about it. It was so weird, so incomprehensible, and I was beginning to grow more afraid of what all this meant.

And just when I was turning and looking more frustrated than ever before in my life, I heard a pair of footsteps coming into the main hall.

For a moment, I took a step back and then I tried to turn and run away, but I realized that that man was probably my only chance of getting out of this mansion. My only chance of doing that because I was growing suspicious that all the other doors and even the windows in the mansion were locked.

He was a little tall, with dark hair, had some beard on his face, and also had a sculpted jawline that could make any man envious of him. His eyes were piercing-blue and were staring attentively at me, almost as if he could read everything that was going on in my mind.

I was afraid of him more than I was of being locked up in this mansion for years. There was an aura around him that told me that he was different, that he was used to doing the most unspeakable of things without feeling an ounce of remorse.

He was certainly not the kind of person that I wanted to even take a step toward. I wanted as much distance between us as possible.

"You can't open any of the doors or the windows," he said,

holding his ground.

His voice was deep and commanding, holding me where I was. It wasn't like I could run anywhere and hide from him in a place whose layout I didn't even know, anyway. He would find me and I didn't even like thinking about what he would do to me if that happened. He looked so strong, well-built, even in his dark and business-y suit.

And there was also the hint of an accent in his voice, though I couldn't put my finger on it.

"Who are you?"

"I could ask you the same," he said and then stepped toward me. I should be running away from him as fast as I could, but his eyes were keeping me frozen in place.

He stopped when he was no more than two feet in front of me and I just realized how much taller than me he truly was. I could bury my head in his chest easily, I thought and, for some reason, that was a huge turn-on.

CHAPTER 2

I figured something odd was going on here, but I never thought I was going to find such a striking and beautiful woman in the mansion. I knew that someone locked me up here, and yet I thought I was alone. I thought I was going to run into whoever was playing this trick on me, and I never thought that that person was none other than this woman, whose name I didn't know.

"Tell me your name," she demanded and even though I could see that she was trying to look braver than normal, I knew that it was nothing more than an act. So much so that I wasn't even slightly afraid of her or what she could do.

"That is at least something I can remember."

"What do you mean?"

"I don't remember how I came to be here, and by the way my name is Iov."

"My name is Ferlisha," she responded and I could feel my dick getting harder in my pants. It wasn't going to tent it up or do anything like that, but it was still getting a little annoying. I knew that I had an instant attraction to her, and yet I never thought it was so strong. It was almost like we had a previous history together and, even though my mind couldn't remember it, my body could. "So that means you don't remember anything as well?"

I shook my head. "I don't. I don't remember how I ended up

here. Someone must have put us here."

"And who could that be?" She asked and we both turned to the right quickly when we heard a pair of footsteps entering the main hall.

It was another man, tall, broad-shouldered, with dark hair, and his beard was made. He appeared to be around the same age I was and wore a suit similar to mine.

Ferlisha wore a wedding dress, which made all this so much more puzzling. Was she getting married when she was kidnapped and then put here? I didn't know, but the question hung in the air like something mean.

"Maybe it's you."

"I heard what you're saying," the man said, stepping toward us and then stopping so that he kept his distance. "And no, I wasn't the one who put you here. I also don't remember anything."

His accent... His voice. I could almost put my finger on it and, yet, I couldn't. It was so difficult to figure out where he came from and what he was doing here, although it wouldn't be too far-fetched to think that he had something to do with the fact that we were here. Maybe he really was the one who kidnapped us, though that would mean that I was beginning to get sloppy.

"How come you also don't remember anything?" Ferlisha asked, putting her hand on her chest.

"I just... don't."

"Do you remember where you're from and what you are doing in the country?"

He turned his eyes to me, narrowing them slightly. "Are you going to tell me what you're doing here?"

I narrowed my eyes slightly as well.

"I don't have to tell you anything." I fisted my hand. There was something about him that made me loathe him even though I didn't know what it was. All I knew was that I hated him with my life. I wanted to kill him and perhaps that's what I came here to do, given my 'profession.'

"Obviously not," he said, shifting his weight. "You're Ferlisha and Iov. I'm Danilo. Danilo Manna."

On the mention of his name, my eyes widened. I didn't think he was that person. He was one of the most important people not just in his country, but also in the whole world.

I didn't know what he was doing here, and it puzzled me that he wasn't accompanied by a whole battalion of bodyguards. They should be around here somewhere, or at least searching for him as much as they could.

"You are the head of the Manna family," I growled, almost remembering that whatever I was doing, wherever I was, had to have something to do with him. Maybe I tried to kill him and failed. Whatever it was that happened, he was in the midst of it, I was sure.

"That I am," he said, and then his hands went into the pocket of his pants. "And I can't find my phone. Do you have yours with you?"

Ferlisha and I both shook our heads. "Whoever put us here, they took our phones as well."

"Figures." He turned his eyes to the right, sighing. "And we need to figure out a way out of here. I don't want to stay another minute with you."

He didn't look at anyone in particular, but I was pretty sure that he was talking about me. It was like there was this intense fire between us and there was nothing we could do about it, other than killing each other. And I wasn't going to try anything without first knowing why I hated him so much and how we could get out of the house.

"All the doors and the windows are shut tight. We can't open them," I said and my words didn't surprise him. If anything, he was already waiting for them.

"I know. Before coming here and finding out that you are also here with me, I noticed that all the doors and the windows are locked. I can't do anything about it, and it is what it is."

"So, what do you suggest we should do?" We heard a voice booming from the other side of the main hall, catching us off-guard. I thought that we were alone, that nobody else was in the mansion with us. Whatever was going on here, it just got a lot weirder.

"Who are you?" Ferlisha squeaked, stepping away from us. Seeing that, I couldn't help but put myself between her and the other guys. I felt this instant urge to protect her against anything and everyone else that was here, and I wasn't going to deny it. As far as my mind knew, I didn't have any history with her, but my body knew better. It was acting on its own.

"I'm Lester Brown, Senator to North Carolina," he responded and bowed with a half-smile on his face. He was mocking us, which only made me feel even more suspicious about his presence. He could be the one that locked us up in here and, if that was the case, he was probably the one that had the key.

"You are a senator?" Danilo asked. "Never heard of you."

He straightened up his back, keeping his half-smile on his face.

"You might have not heard about me until now, but it doesn't matter. We need to find out what happened here." He took a couple of steps toward us. "And don't worry about telling me your names. I overheard you talking before."

"Of course you did."

Ferlisha stepped forward until she was between us, still looking so stunning and a little silly in her wedding dress. "Now that we are here and together, maybe we can find a way out."

"Sure, if you have something that could blow open one of the doors. I don't have anything on me," Lester replied, his tone still sounding a little mocking and also a little too happy for my liking.

His eyes were jade-green and his hair was blond. He was the only one in here that looked… Well, I wasn't even going to say it.

"Obviously, we don't have anything for that," I said. "We need to figure out something, though."

"Let's go somewhere else. I imagine that we can think better in a place that isn't so open and looks so well-unguarded," Danilo said and we followed him, finding the dining room.

It was big and spacious, with a huge table sitting in the middle of it. It didn't look dusty or old, which meant that someone had been using this mansion before we were dragged here. Whoever that was, they were probably behind our kidnapping.

"Happy that we are here now?" Lester asked, his voice a little too cheerful for my liking. I wanted to punch his face so hard that it was impossible to put it into words. I didn't know what was about it, but I hated everyone in this room minus Ferlisha. She was the only one I wanted to protect and to see well after we got out of here. And after that happened – because it was going to – I would stay in touch with her.

"It's better," Danilo replied, glancing around and then his eyes widened when he realized that there was something on the table.

He picked it up and I noticed that it was a piece of paper. It was white, torn at the sides, and something was written on it. I couldn't read it from where I was and I wasn't going to get any-where nearer to Danilo than I already was.

He was going to have to read whatever it said to us.

CHAPTER 3

Danilo

I figured something odd was going on here, but I didn't think I was going to find this piece of paper that I was now holding in my hand. There was something written on it and, for a moment, I thought it was just a joke. It should be, right? Whoever was doing this was probably just playing a trick on us.

"Well, are you going to read it or not?" Lester asked and, suddenly, his voice sounded a lot thicker and a lot less cheerful. I didn't know what was about it, but he appeared to be more serious. Out of everyone in the dining room, he was the one I was thinking probably had something to do with our kidnapping.

I grunted, saying out loud, "I'm so happy that you're here and that you've finally found this letter. It means that you aren't as stupid as I thought you were. It also means that you have to do exactly what I want. You don't know anything about this, at least not until now, but Ferlisha was getting married. She looked so happy when it was happening.

So much so that I was angry with her. I wanted to kill her, but not anymore. I've come up with this and it's a much more elegant solution. And yet, I don't want it to end here. I want Ferlisha to find out, who between you three, she was getting married to."

I put the piece of paper down on the table, my hand shaking slightly. I couldn't believe what I just read. I figured that Ferlisha might have been getting married before she wound up here, but I didn't think that it really was the case.

I thought that it was thanks to something else, perhaps that it was Halloween and that she was partying at one of her friends' before she was kidnapped.

"Tell me that this is some kind of joke," Iov said, stepping toward me and looking at me with serious eyes. I didn't know what was about him, but he looked so threatening that he made me slightly afraid of him, though not much more than that. I'd dealt with worse.

"It's not. I would never joke about this," I said and he picked up the piece of paper, reading what was on it. The fact that he then grunted and didn't say anything else told me that he wasn't the one behind this.

I was thinking that, if there was someone who kidnapped us, it could be one of us, too. It was a possibility and one that I was already dearly considering.

He put the piece of paper down on the table and Lester picked it up. Ferlisha was by my side and I was the one protecting her, though I could tell that the other guys were also trying to distance myself from her. I figured that they were beginning to feel the same thing that I felt for her.

She was stunning. Chocolate skin, caramel eyes, a little chubby, but so incredibly curvy I just wanted to explore every part of her body, loving her. I knew that we didn't have the time for that, but when we were out of here, it was probably going to be one of the first things that I was going to do. Actually, scratch that. It was going to be the very first.

It only sucked that it was going to take so long until then.

"I'll be damned," Lester said, crumpling the paper in his hand and then tossing it over his head. "And we don't need this shit anymore. I'm not going to do anything about any wedding or whatever it was that the piece of paper said. I just want to get out of here, go back to Washington DC, and go back to my life. I've got so many things to do and I don't have any time for whatever is going on here."

"If you have anything you want to say, any idea on how to get out of here, I'm all ears," I said, locking my eyes with his and hoping that he was going to come up with something. He looked stupid, but he couldn't be too stupid. At least, that's what I was thinking. He was a little unusual and a little too cheerful, but the fact that he was paired with me and Iov meant that he was as smart as we were.

"I don't know how to do that," he said, stepping away from us and then out of the dining room.

When he was out of sight, I asked, "Where are you going? You know that there's nothing else that you can do here and nowhere else where you can go."

"I don't know. I just don't want to be in the same place as you."

I shook my head, nearing Ferlisha. Whatever was going on here, I needed to keep her safe, especially from someone like Iov. I didn't know who he was, but something about him told me that he was more than what met the eye.

So much so that I was already thinking if I shouldn't just kill him, even though I didn't have my knife or gun. Whoever put us here in this mansion, they got rid of those things, too. We didn't even have our phones, not that it mattered anyway. We wouldn't be able to call anyone from where we were.

"We should keep an eye on him," Iov mentioned and I nodded. I knew he was right, but I didn't want to say it out loud.

"We should, but I'm not going anywhere."

"We should focus on finding a way out of here."

"Perhaps, but I just want to make sure that nobody is going to kill me. It's dark, I'm a little hungry, and I want to find out what else is in this mansion. I think that there might be other pieces of paper scattered around in here."

"You think so?" Iov asked, refusing to step away from me. His eyes kept looking at Ferlisha, and I was pretty sure that it meant he had a crush on her as well. But if that was the case, I knew that I couldn't let him anywhere near her.

"Yeah. I'm going to see what I can find."

"Then I'm going with you."

A moment of silence and I didn't know what to do. All I knew was that I didn't want him following us, even though I couldn't impede him from doing that. If I wanted to do that, I would have to kill him, which was something that I didn't know I was ready for. Not to mention the mess that it would make and that Ferlisha would think that I was a monster.

"Alright. I guess there's no helping it." I turned to Ferlisha and then asked, "Are you okay? You haven't said anything in a while."

"Yeah, I'm fine." She shook her head, pushing a lock of her hair behind her right ear. I watched as she did that and it happened almost like it was in slow motion. Everything she did was perfect, each movement delicate, and it made my dick a little harder than it already was in my pants. "I'm just a little concerned about everything."

"That's normal. You should be, but don't worry about it. I'm going to keep you safe, no matter what."

Upon saying that, it was like her eyes were glinting. I wanted to be closer to her, to have her in my arms, but I couldn't do that, especially when Iov was still with us and his eyes were trained on me. And it wasn't just that, but also the fact that he was staring at me as if he had the intention of killing me.

"Thanks," she said and her voice was so gentle that it made my crush on her even stronger than it was. I thought that it couldn't happen, but it did. It was the first time in my life, ever since the death of my wife, that I was feeling like this.

I turned to Iov again and said, "Well, shall we go?"

"Yeah," he replied and we stepped out of the dining room. We explored the house as much as we could and we even ran into Lester a couple of times, and he always said that he also didn't find anything, even though it was difficult to find out if he told us the truth or not.

It was possible that he was hiding something from us, just like I was hiding everything about myself from them.

CHAPTER 4

The water moving down over my body was excellent, warm, and perfect. I was in one of the bathrooms of the house and everything around me was quiet. I couldn't hear anything happening anywhere in the house, other than the sound of the howling wind seeping through the cracks.

We explored everything, every nook and cranny, but didn't find anything other than that small piece of paper. Whoever wrote that shit, he had something coming. I wasn't going to remain jailed here for long.

I mean, there was Ferlisha, but the other guys were hounding her and it didn't appear that they were going to stop doing that anytime soon. Ferlisha was beautiful and unlike all the women that I always met in the world of politics.

They were usually old, decrypt, and with their boobs sagging and looking a little empty. Ferlisha was so much better. She was a little fat, but there was nothing wrong with that.

In fact, she was so beautiful the way she was. I wouldn't change anything about her, which was something I wanted to tell her, even though I didn't have the time to do that.

I was soaping up my shoulder when I dropped the bath sponge, noticing that my dick was so hard that I had to loop my fingers around it and start to stroke it. I was doing that slowly, taking my time, and at the moment forgetting that I was taking a shower.

I had no idea where everyone else was, but I was thinking about Ferlisha and her going down to her knees, wrapping her lips around my cock, and taking it all in.

I'd come in her mouth and she would swallow everything. I could just imagine that happening, and I would do it even while we were still in this shitty house.

I didn't know if anyone here liked this kind of style, but it wasn't for me. Too old, moldy, and everything in it smelled of farts and garlic.

The more I thought about it, the more I hated it. The only thing that was keeping me sane here was Ferlisha and she was nowhere to be found.

I figured that because it was dark and she was probably sleepy that she had to be sleeping in one of the rooms, but I wasn't going to go out looking for her.

Whoever built this place, did it to last. It was impossible to break down the doors or shatter the windows without proper equipment, and I tried doing both of those things several times before I gave up.

I was picking up the pace, my hand shooting up and down along my dick, and I could feel the heat rising in my body. I could feel my balls slapping against my hands and even though this was something that I usually didn't do, I was making an exception because Ferlisha was just that stunning. She was everywhere in my mind and I couldn't erase her from it, even if I was trying to.

But then I opened my eyes, checked my surroundings carefully, and moved my hand away from my dick. What was I even doing? I asked myself, feeling like I wasn't being myself.

I didn't jerk off anymore. I was rich, influential, and pretty much every woman I knew always fell to her knees when meeting me. With Ferlisha, it shouldn't be any different. I knew she would be doing the same if we were alone.

I would never even think about killing Iov and Danilo, but now

I wished I could. Regardless, when I was out of here, I was going to stay in touch with Ferlisha, and Danilo and Iov could go to jail for all I cared. It was a promise that I was making to myself.

I let the water flow around my body and remove the soap and the foam, stepping out of the shower cubicle moments later. Then I went to where I left my clothes.

I just picked up my shirt when the door of the bathroom opened all of a sudden and in stepped none other than Ferlisha herself.

I widened my eyes, but didn't try to hide my junk. Why would I do that when I wasn't ashamed of it or anything of the sort? But she covered her eyes with her right hand at the same moment, turning around and leaving the bathroom.

"Wait, don't go," I said, lifting my hand as if I was trying to grab her even though I was dozens of feet away from her.

She stopped just like I thought she was going to, but didn't turn around to meet my eyes, which was a little annoying. I wanted to see her pretty face again. Her back, even though it was a part of her that I wanted to feel with my hands, wasn't enough.

"I'm sorry. I didn't know there was someone in the bathroom."

"I didn't think you were just going to open the door without checking for that."

"I was a little careless, I know. It won't happen again."

A moment of silence as I checked her out from bottom to top, delineating her curves with my eyes. There was something about her body that I just couldn't put into words, and it was maddening.

"You should put your clothes back on."

"Should I?" And I noticed that my prick was hard again. I couldn't stop thinking about doing all kinds of unspeakable things with Ferlisha, and I was pretty sure that at least a part of her was thinking the same thing. She had to be. I was never wrong about the intentions of a woman.

"You know, I don't know you well, but you seem kind of a jerk," she said without turning around to meet my eyes, even though she should.

"Urgh, this is so annoying," I said, tossing my shirt and then going to her, stopping right behind her.

"What do you think you're doing?" She asked, suddenly whirling around and meeting my eyes. They were fiery and determined, just like I hoped they were going to be. If there was something I enjoyed, it was a tough woman trying to pretend that she had any chance against me.

Not to mention that I could see in her eyes how much lust she was feeling for me right now. It was everywhere in her eyes and they were even gleaming with it.

"I'm just making sure that I'm not getting mixed signals here," I explained, and even though I knew it was inappropriate to be this close to a woman while I was butt naked, it wasn't like she wasn't enjoying it. If anything, she was loving it! This was the first time she was in a situation like this one, wasn't she?

"What mixed signals?" She asked and her eyes went up and down, checking me out. I was quite different from her. My skin was milk-white, my hair blond, and she was a perfect representation of a stunning African-American.

"You know what I'm talking about."

"I don't," she said and I noticed that her voice was sounding like a whisper now. It was quite different from the voice that I had heard before and especially when she was trying to sound tough.

"Do you really want me to put my clothes on?" I asked, moving a little closer to her and finding it a little annoying that she was still with her marriage dress on. I had no idea why she hadn't taken it off already, though maybe she didn't find anything she could wear, too.

She opened and closed her mouth several times, looking like a goldfish. A cute, sweet goldfish, and one that I wanted to do all kinds of things with.

"I mean, we're in this really big house, it's shitty, but the walls are thick and nobody would hear anything. You're beautiful and you keep looking at my cock. We could do it and none of the other guys would find out about it."

She opened and closed her mouth several times, making me shake my head and shut her lips with my finger.

"You don't need to say anything. Let's go with me to my room, I'll lock the door, and then you can tell me what you want to do. Deal?" I asked, hoping she was going to give me the right answer.

She nodded once and slowly, and then I looped my arm around her body, going with her to my bedroom after picking up my clothes.

I knew she was going to fall to her knees before me.

CHAPTER 5

Ferlisha

I didn't think that I was going to stumble into him stark naked in the bathroom and much less that he had a crush on me. I mean, ever since we first met, I noticed he was always stealing glances at me, but I never thought that he had such strong feelings for me.

So much so that I was still a little surprised that we were going to his bedroom, that he just locked the door with a key, and that he was still butt naked and was no more than a handful of feet across from me.

I knew I had a thing for dominating, white jerks like him, but I thought I was stronger than this.

I should be feeling ashamed of myself, but the possibility of having my first time with a man kept on being a thought in my mind that I couldn't erase, and it was burning hot in it. I couldn't control it and I didn't have a mental fire extinguisher for it, and I knew that stopping what was unraveling before my eyes was a lost cause, too.

"Now that the door is locked, we can do anything we want, princess," he said, tossing the key to the side and it fell on a couch. His room was quite spacious and big. There was enough space in it for the king-sized bed that was behind me, and desks and bookcases as well. I felt so tiny in here, especially in the presence of someone that was probably around 6'5" and heavier than me.

"Princess? I can't be that much younger than you."

"You're always going to be my princess, whether you like it or not," he said, stepping toward me and I noticed that his dick kept on swinging in front of his legs, his balls bouncing up and down. It was the first time that I was alone in a room with a man and I had no idea what to do. Would it be a turnoff if he found out that I was a virgin? I asked myself and I decided to keep that hidden.

When he was no more than 2 feet from me, I stepped away from him and said, "Wait. Iov and Danilo are going to start looking for me and when they realize I'm here, they'll be so angry. I don't want to anger them."

He put both of his hands on my face, tilting it up and making my eyes lock with his. His hands weren't callous or rough. They were quite gentle, like the hands of someone that never had to lift anything heavy in his life. Given that he was a senator, that only made sense.

"Don't think about them and don't make me remember that they exist. They want you as well, but they can't have you."

What he said was hot, thrilling, and exactly what I always thought someone like him would say. He was a jerk, overconfident, and always thinking so highly of himself, and I was falling for his trap and couldn't do anything about it.

I looked down, assessing the size of his prick. It was so thick I was wondering if my hand was big enough. Chances were it wasn't.

He smirked, the breath coming out of his mouth minty and intoxicating. I didn't know if he brushed his teeth before I stumbled into him in the bathroom, but it was almost like he did. It made me want to kiss him, but I had no idea if he wanted to do something that looked so… romantic. I didn't think that he was the romantic type.

He studied my eyes and my expression, reading what I was thinking, and it was only obvious that it was going to happen. I closed my eyes, waited for our lips to touch, and I wasn't surprised when they did. His lips were so gentle and yet also a little rough when it happened, and I loved that.

Lester dug his tongue into my mouth, making me moonwalk until my back hit the wall. I couldn't do anything about it and I was just annoyed that I was still with my wedding dress on. I tried to find a new set of clothes to put on, but couldn't. There was nothing in any of the closets and wardrobes in the mansion, and it was pointless to keep looking.

I didn't even try to battle against his tongue because I knew it was pointless. Our kiss was extremely passionate from the get-go, his lips rubbing against mine, devouring my mouth, and there was nothing that could be done about it. I melted in his arms and I knew he was aware of that. I knew that it turned him on more than he already was.

Then, he broke the kiss, taking his time to analyze what his eyes were seeing. He was checking out my face and my expression, trying to figure out if I liked the kiss. There wasn't much to figure out, though. It was obvious that I loved it.

"You kiss well for someone with zero experience," he said, making my heart speed up even more than it already was. My heart was beating like a jackhammer in my chest and there was nothing I could do about it. It was only doing what it was supposed to be doing.

"How did you know?" I asked, even though the answer to the question was quite obvious. A womanizer, overconfident jerk like him was always going to figure that out without much effort.

"I knew about it before we kissed, when we first met in the main hall."

"That can't be possible. I don't think I kiss that bad."

"There are so many things about you that you don't really know," he said, turning me around and then until he laid me down on his bed, widening the gap between my legs with his hands and pushing up the lower part of my wedding dress.

"You really didn't find anything else that you can wear?" He asked and I shook my head. He pinched the band of my panties with both hands, lowered them, and then said, "You shaved. Were you thinking you were going to have your wedding night with one of us?"

"I don't even know who my husband is supposed to be," I croaked and he purred, sliding his hands along my legs, feeling them and loving my skin. He knew how to apply the right amount of pressure and where.

"Well, how about finding out the truth soon with me? I'm pretty sure that only I can do what I'm going to do now," he purred again, approaching his head to the gap between my legs and studying my pussy for what felt like hours.

He was such a jerk, especially that he was taking so long to do what needed to be done, what he was teasing he was going to do.

"I don't know."

"You don't know?" He growled, sticking his tongue out and then giving my cunt a long, powerful lick that sent shivers down my spine. I didn't think he was going to be like this, that he was going to be giving me so much pleasure.

I had no idea if he truly was my husband, but part of me was hoping he was, even though I didn't think that marrying such a jerk was a good idea. "Then, there's no point in going on with this."

He was moving away from me when I pleaded, "Please, don't go."

"Changing your mind already?" He asked, settling his hands on my waist and giving my snatch a flurry of licks, and sometimes they were slow and ever-lasting. I couldn't help but move my hand down, find my clit with my finger, and then start rubbing it until I felt like I was going to come.

"I don't know."

He shook his head before he said, "You are annoying me with all your 'I don't know.' You should make up your mind about it."

I tilted my head and arched my back when he continued his

assault with his tongue against my flower, and I kept on rubbing my clit. He was going to make me come.

Lester was going to make me reach my climax and there was nothing I could do to stop it. I needed the release that was going to come with that, and I was pretty sure he was more than willing to give me that.

I felt my breathing quickening, my hips bucked, and sweat was pooling on my forehead when it all happened. My body convulsed slightly, and I knew that it was the best orgasm that ever happened in my life. Even my hand was slightly sore after what happened.

And I was just catching my breath when I heard footsteps nearing us.

CHAPTER 6

"Think I heard something coming from that room," I said, pointing to it with my finger. Danilo was by my side and we had been searching everywhere in the mansion for a way to get out of it, but we couldn't. It was a fruitless endeavor, and it looked like the only way of making that happen was by finding out who Ferlisha's husband was.

I was hoping that it was me, but I wondered if I even had time for that. I wondered if I'd had enough time to fall in love, to think that she was the right one, and that I was going to retire.

I thought I never would, given that my life was always circling around that part of it. I was an assassin, worked for Walter Group, and I couldn't just start a new life outside of it, right?

We stopped in front of the door and I put my ear against it, trying to hear if anything else was happening behind it. When I heard the sounds and noises of someone putting their clothes on, I knew that it had to be Lester. Maybe Ferlisha was here as well? I didn't know, but my heart was tight at the thought. I didn't want to find out that they were already doing things behind my back, that I was losing her to him. It would hurt me so much if that were the case, and I didn't even want to think about it.

"There's someone in there," I said, trying the doorknob and when it didn't turn, I wasn't surprised. I figured that whoever was in the room had locked the door with the key.

"Let me try to kick it down," Danilo offered, but even he didn't think that it was possible. The door was thick, heavy, and just like everything else in the house, we couldn't damage it. There was something to be said about old constructions like this one. People in those times didn't half-ass them, I thought.

He was already lifting his foot when I heard someone approaching the door, using the key in the keyhole, and then they turned the doorknob. The door opened and I wasn't surprised when I found Lester on the other side.

He was leaning against the doorway with his arm and his head propped on his hand. He had a mocking smile on his face, as if he was finding it amusing that we were here.

"Good night, boys. I didn't think I was going to find you here, and much less at this time of the night."

"Have you seen Ferlisha somewhere?" I asked, my heart feeling a little tight. As an assassin, I was always cold and calculative, but now things were different. I was disconcerted by the fact that Ferlisha was probably somewhere in the room, maybe even in the adjacent bathroom.

He shook his head slowly and once. "No, sorry. Can't say I did."

"Can't or won't?" Danilo asked, stepping into the room without Lester's permission. And even though I couldn't see Ferlisha anywhere in here, I knew that she was, or at least that she had been here until not too long ago. After all, I could smell her perfume and her body odor in the air.

"I haven't seen her anywhere since I left you in the dining room," he explained and I knew that it was bullshit. So much so that I was already checking out every nook and cranny in the room, going to his bed.

There was some space under it and if there was a place where she was, then it could be there, even though that would mean that she was dirtying her dress and pretty skin.

Not to mention that she would be putting herself in a very humiliating position and would be hiding from us, which was something that I didn't even want to be thinking about.

I stopped by the bed and when I was going to look under it, Lester said, "Hey, what do you think you're doing? This is my room and you can't just go and snoop around."

I turned to look at him, asking, "You really don't know where Ferlisha is?"

"I don't and I suggest we go out to look for her. After all, we don't even know where we are and she could be in danger, don't you agree?"

He was a slippery one and his proposal made sense. I should go along with it, except that I could still feel that Ferlisha was somewhere in the room. The fact that Lester didn't want me to look under the bed was suspicious, to say the least.

"I agree, but not right now. If you are hiding something from me, then you should tell me everything. Especially if it means it could help us get out of here."

"I'm not hiding anything from you, as I said." He smiled, waving his hand. "If you want to look under the bed, then do it. I'm pretty sure you aren't going to find Ferlisha there."

I narrowed my eyes slightly, knelt with just one knee, and then looked under the bed. For a moment, I thought I was going to find her there, but I was surprised when I didn't. I could still feel the smell of her perfume in the room, and I was still suspicious.

I stood up, straightening my back.

"If you haven't seen Ferlisha again, then why can I smell her perfume everywhere in the room?" I asked and that made Danilo shift his weight, showing me that he also felt the same thing. He could feel her perfume, that it was that everywhere, and Lester couldn't hide it.

The fact that it was still impregnating the air in the room showed me that it hadn't been long since she was here. And after I found her, I was going to have so many questions for her it was going to be overwhelming.

He pursed his lips, shaking his head. "I don't know." He sniffed the air, looking around and then also under the bed. "I think you're probably imagining things."

"I'm pretty sure I'm not imagining anything."

Danilo put himself between us, looking at me and then Lester.

"This isn't helping with anything and it's pretty obvious that Ferlisha isn't here," he said, opening the door of the bathroom and checking it. She was also not in there, and I expected that she wasn't.

But an old house like this one probably had several hidden rooms, so maybe she was in one of them, which wouldn't be surprising. She wouldn't want me or Danilo to find out that she was getting more intimate with Lester, especially now that it was obvious we were all falling for her.

"Then, let's go out. There's no point staying in here longer than we have to," I said, going out of the room when I heard someone sneezing behind me and it couldn't be any of us. It had to be Ferlisha, and it was everything I needed right now.

"Who just sneezed?" I asked and Lester opened a big, bright smile on his face. And if he was thinking that it was going to be enough to fool me, then he had something coming.

"Sneezed?" He said, stepping toward me and looking more serious all of a sudden. "You probably just imagined it."

"I'm pretty sure that's not it," I growled and he was right in front of me this time, trying to look more threatening, but it wasn't working. I had faced people much worse than him, and it was obvious that he didn't know anything about my reputation. Otherwise, he wouldn't be feeling so overconfident.

"No, I'm certain I heard something, too," Danilo said, stepping to one of the bookshelves and then checking out the books. His finger slid over a bump, he pressed it, and a portion of the adjacent wall slid open to the side, revealing none other than Ferlisha herself.

I knew that from the very beginning she was hidden here

somewhere, but I didn't think that it was in the walls. I thought that she was hidden in a room that we couldn't access.

She looked dirty and dusty, coughing as she stepped back into the room. Waving her hands in front of her, she tried to say that she was sorry about this, but it was pointless.

It wasn't going to change the fact that she was with Lester much before she had the chance of being with me, and that was competition, and I didn't like it.

"Ooopsie," Lester joked, stepping so that he was by her side. "Looks like you caught me lying."

CHAPTER 7

Danilo

I figured that Iov was right about Ferlisha being here some-where, but I never thought that she was hidden in the wall. It was a little disgusting, but at least she was safe and with us. She was right by my side and I knew that she needed my help. So much so that I didn't hold back before putting my arm around her and taking her to the bed, even though it was obvious that neither Iov nor Lester liked that.

Well, they could do whatever they wanted about it. It wasn't going to stop me, especially when it was about this stunning woman.

"Are you okay? You shouldn't be hiding in places like that," I warned, moving my hand on her shoulders so that she felt more comfortable.

Eventually, she stopped coughing, turning her eyes up so that she was looking at me. I could see a glint of something in her eyes, and it was endearing and it made me feel even crazier for her.

"Yes, thank you. Thank you for worrying about me."

"It's okay. It's not my job, but I'll take care of you, no matter what. Not to mention that we just found out that Lester was lying about your whereabouts, and that's not something I can forgive. I can't put up with it."

"Whoa, what's going on here now?" Lester said, coming toward us, but a glance was enough to make him stop. After all, even though he was influential and overconfident, he stood no chance against me. I was a Don of a mafia family and I needed people like him to respect me, especially because, when it came to politicians, they were only good when they were under my command. "You can't just start touching her like that."

"And? What are you going to do about it?" I asked, wondering if he was going to do anything, but then finding it unsurprising when he didn't.

I had my arm over Ferlisha's shoulders and I wasn't going to move it anywhere. As far as I was concerned, she was a little disconcerted about having to hide in the wall, and she needed to be as far away from Lester as possible.

Turning my head so that I was looking at her again, I asked, "Wanna leave? This room is filthy and you deserve to be somewhere better." I turned my head so that I locked my eyes with Iov's and I couldn't read his expression. It was cold, calculative, and pensive. "Are you okay with that too?"

"Do whatever you want," he said, going out of the room and then adding, "I'm going to figure out a way out of this place."

Lester and I didn't say anything as we watched him leaving the premises, and then I was alone with Ferlisha and him. I wondered if he was going to continue being stupid about it, but when I realized that he wasn't going to do anything, I smiled.

My smile was enough to show him that I wasn't kidding about this. He had his chance with Ferlisha and I wasn't going to let her anywhere near him again.

I lowered my arm so that it was around her waist, standing up with her as we went out of the room, too. "I'm going to take you somewhere better, where nobody is forcing you to do anything."

Lester opened his mouth, but didn't say anything. He was harmless as far as I was concerned and that wasn't going to change anytime soon. I didn't think that Iov was suddenly going to find a way out of the house, after all.

Ferlisha craned her head so that she was looking at me, saying, "Thanks. I really don't know what got into me when I decided to go along with it. I shouldn't have tried to hide in that wall."

"No, you really shouldn't have," I affirmed, walking with her to my bedroom, opening it, and watching as she sat on the bed. "And we really need to find something for you to wear. That wedding dress is annoying me."

"Really?" She asked, sounding a little disappointed. "Then that probably means you can't be my husband."

Oh, right. There was still that thing. I still needed to find out if I was her husband – or was going to be – before we were put in this house. It was something for another time, I thought. Right now, I just wanted to focus on us, on finding out more about her.

I was tired and ready to take a shower. I wasn't too keen about spending more time in this house than needed, but for the time being, there was no way around it. Not to mention that I just wanted to return to my old life, where I could do anything and everything I wanted without having to worry about what two other guys thought about it.

I took off my shirt and I wasn't surprised when I noticed Ferlisha checking me out. I figured that she was going to, especially because she could be plenty of things, but one of them certainly wasn't that she was naïve or innocent.

She wanted me as well, didn't she? It wasn't even a question. It was more like an affirmation of something that I could see with my eyes.

I turned around and I could see that she was checking out my tattoos. When a second passed and she didn't say anything, I decided to say, "Curious about them?"

She threaded her fingers through her hair, looking a little disconcerted and uncomfortable all of a sudden. I knew that it didn't make sense that we were going to do this especially after I showed how angry I was when I found out that she was having sex with Lester, but my body thought otherwise.

It was what it wanted and I couldn't control it, especially because I didn't want to look like a pussy if she thought that I wasn't man enough for her. Not to mention that having a one-night stand with her wouldn't be the end of the world.

"You have so many of them."

I put my shirt on the nightstand, where it wasn't going to get in our way. I sat on the bed and I could tell that it made her feel even more nervous than she was. After all, she couldn't stop moving her fingers against each other, her hands clasped on her lap.

"I had to go through so many things to get where I am."

"Iov said that you are a mafia boss. When I first looked at you, I knew it was possible, but I didn't want to think that it was true."

"Why is that?" I asked, shifting closer to her, this time feeling more strongly the perfume that still exuded from her body. It was intoxicating and I knew she was aware of that. It was the main reason why she was wearing it for the wedding, wasn't it?

"It scares me."

I lowered my eyelids slightly, softening my expression.

"You don't need to worry about it or me. You don't need to be scared of it. I'm not dangerous to you."

"That doesn't change anything. If I was going to get married, then I don't think that my father or anyone else in my life wanted that. They couldn't have allowed it."

I caressed her cheek with my hand, feeling how soft and smooth her skin was. I didn't know how she managed it, but it was like the skin of someone much younger. Ferlisha was so perfect in the way she was and that was something she should always keep in mind.

"You don't know that. I've seen so many arranged marriages in my life, and I know something terrible happened that you don't want to talk about. This isn't about what I think that they made us drink so that we forgot."

"What?" She was saying, but the expression on her face was already too telling. She wanted me to do this, she wanted me to kiss her, and I was more than willing to make that real. So much so that our lips connected and she didn't do anything about it, though I could feel that she was a little conflicted about it.

I supposed that it was so because she'd been with Lester not too long ago and was worried that he was going to find out about this. But he couldn't. I locked the door and nobody was going to dare open it and stop what was happening.

I didn't use my tongue and our kiss was passionate and slow at the same time. She was loving it and I knew she didn't want it to stop anytime soon. When I reopened my eyes, I noticed that her eyes were still closed, which I imagined wasn't going to change anytime soon.

When it felt like hours since our lips connected, we finally broke the kiss and I noticed that her eyes were going up and down, checking me out.

"So, what do you say?" I asked, pressing my torso slightly against her and getting a little annoyed that she was still with her wedding dress on. We really needed to find something else she could wear. "Do you think I'm your husband or fiancé or whatever?"

"It's possible…" She murmured and then she added, "but I'm only going to be sure after we do one more thing."

"Are you really thinking what I'm thinking?" I asked and I knew that it was a question that wasn't going to be answered. So much so that I was already bringing her down against the bed and then straddling her, our lips connecting one more time.

If there was something that I was going to show her, it was that I was much better than Lester at what we were doing.

CHAPTER 8

Ferlisha

I didn't think that I was going to hop from one womanizer, overconfident asshole, and then fall into the arms of another. Danilo was all over me, kissing me, dominating me, and making me melt under him. And he wasn't stopping or showing any signs that he was going to do that anytime soon. He was relentless from the get-go, his hands desperate to feel more and more of me.

"God, you're amazing," he murmured against my lips, digging his tongue in and I did nothing to stop him. I knew that it was pointless and that it would lead nowhere. I was a little disappointed when he and Iov ruined what I was having with Lester, but I wasn't going to hold a grudge. If anything, this was his chance to make up for it.

I wanted to say something, but his tongue was inside my mouth and there was nothing I could do about it. I was only thinking that, if I were his wife, then what was I thinking when I decided to get married to a mafioso? After all, was I really okay with putting my life at risk that way? I didn't know. I couldn't remember anything about that.

All I knew was that he was relentless and wasn't going to stop for anything right now.

I could hear his huffs, feel his hands moving over my legs, pushing up my dress. He got rid of my panties and when I thought he was going to start devouring my pussy, he was already some-where else. He was focusing on kneading and massaging my thick thighs with his massive hands, and I loved it.

"I don't know what happened between you and Lester, but a pussy like him doesn't deserve you," he growled, kissing my neck and then my cheek, lowering the front zipper of my dress and being all over me in such a way that it was difficult to breathe.

I felt like I was running out of air, but I still didn't say anything about that. I just wanted to keep grinding my body against his, to keep loving him the way this was happening, and wondering if, by doing this, I was going to figure out if he was my husband or not. Or fiancé, or whatever. The appropriate term was pointless.

"Do you want me to get rid of this?" He asked, obviously refer-ring to my dress and I couldn't help but nod. I was always going to do that, especially because it was what he wanted.

"Yes, please," I murmured and he helped me out of my wedding dress. When I wasn't wearing it anymore, I felt so much freer and like I could do anything, including losing my virginity to him. I was pretty sure that Danilo was thinking the same thing, as well.

His eyes scanned me and then he said, "Oh gosh, you're so beautiful, especially without your wedding dress."

I never thought that I was going to have someone so hand-some and much older than me saying that, but here it was. And Danilo wasn't ashamed of himself, was he? Glancing at him, I couldn't see any signs of that, and I didn't think they were going to show up all of a sudden, either.

He started to kiss and love my belly, moving his hand over it as he made me feel even more vulnerable. I felt a little exposed without my panties on, but it was no surprise that he was already looking for the most important prize for him. He wanted it and he was going to have it.

He moved down, putting his tongue out and licking my pussy. Then, Danilo looked up, finding my eyes as he asked, "He didn't get this far with you, did he?"

I weighed my answer. I knew that he was looking for only one answer, and I didn't want to give him the wrong one. If I did, he would be so pissed that he could even kill Lester, and I didn't want to have that weight on my shoulders. I wasn't going to.

And so, I just shook my head quickly and it was enough to fool him. When he was content with the answer he got, he continued licking and sliding his tongue over my pussy, his hand going up and then finding my clit. I knew he was going to do that and thus I wasn't surprised when he started to rub it, exciting it beyond any level I thought possible.

I could feel my orgasm coming up, growing in intensity, and I knew that it was going to wash over me like someone threw a bucket of water over me. I was so certain of that I was already preparing myself for it. I didn't want it to be so strong that it would make me pass out. I wanted to remain right here, right where I was, and I was going to make that happen.

"I don't know, but I feel like you just lied to me," he murmured, giving my pussy one last lick before moving back up so that he could put his fingers around the bands of my bra. He circled them around me, unsnapped it, and then pulled it up and over my head.

This time, nothing else was protecting me against him and I wanted things to remain this way. I didn't want anything to get between us.

And regardless of what happened now, the only other thing that I was craving at the moment was finding out how big he was. My mind was filthy like that and I wasn't going to hide it. After all, so few things in life were better.

Not to mention that I was curious if his dick was bigger than Lester's. I wouldn't be surprised if he was.

I didn't think this was going to lead anywhere once I found out who the fiancé was. No way that I thought that getting married to one of those guys was a good idea. I hated politicians, hated criminals, and Iov looked like someone I should never even anger. He could ruin me with his stare alone.

"Thinking about something?" Danilo asked and I didn't know if I should even answer that. I didn't want him to feel disappointed in me, that I was still thinking about the man that he considered his competition.

"No, nothing," I hissed and it was enough to make him smirk.

"Good. You shouldn't be. You should only be thinking about me, about us, and that we might just be perfect for each other."

Danilo really was beginning to feel something strong for me and I didn't know how to take that. All I knew was that he was proficient at what he was doing, and I was loving every second of it.

He lowered his head and wrapped his lips around my left nipple, moving his tongue around it and doing everything else he could with it.

He was so proficient that he was always hitting every spot that he could and was bringing me so much closer to my climax that I knew that, when it hit me, it was going to be one of the strongest that ever happened in my life.

He lifted his head and then moved so that he encircled my other nipple with his lips and started to love it and do everything else he could. His arms were around me, keeping me close to his body and I could feel how warm it was, even though the room was a little cold thanks to the dropping temperatures outside.

When he was done with that nipple as well, he moved so that his face was right in front of me and I could feel that same strong feeling that he felt for me. Danilo wanted me, he wanted to come inside of me, and there was little that I could do against that.

But then, we heard the sound of a gunshot coming from not too far and we both went upright, fearing that the worst just happened in the house. I didn't know what it was, but I was worried and needed to find out the truth behind it.

"What was that?" I asked, putting my underwear and dress back on, feeling a little disappointed and angry that yet one more thing impeded me from having full-blown sex for the first time. I thought that it was finally going to happen, that I was going to find out how great it could be, and I was a little disappointed that this happened.

Regardless, it was time to go out and figure out why someone just fired a gun in the house.

CHAPTER 9

Iov

Holding the gun in my hand, I had fired at the doorknob and I thought it was going to work, that it was going to open the door, but it didn't, and I was disappointed at that. I just found this gun and I thought it was going to solve my problems, only to realize that it was pointless.

But not entirely so. It wasn't pointless in the sense that I couldn't use it for anything. It was going to give me an edge over the other guys and that was valuable. So much so that it was already bringing a smile to my face, even though it was something that I rarely did.

And when I heard footsteps coming into the room, I knew that I'd just gotten the attention of who I needed.

I turned around, meeting none other than Lester himself. His eyes were wide and he was surprised at what my hand was holding. He didn't think that I was going to find anything that was going to give me an edge over him, much less that it was going to be a gun.

"Where did you find that?" He asked, stepping toward me, and I didn't point my gun at him. As far as I was concerned, I didn't come here to kill him. First, I needed to find out what my purpose in the country was. I knew that it was going to take a while, but I could make it happen.

I didn't say anything and then he stopped walking toward me, putting his hands on his waist and then shaking his head.

"Figures that this is happening. Now you have a gun and I don't have anything. I need to find at least a knife so that I can protect myself."

I didn't say anything, noticing that having an argument with him of any sort right now was pointless. He wasn't the kind of person that even listened to anything I had to say. Not to mention that he was always so full of himself that he could only listen to what he had to say.

"And yet, it doesn't help me. I don't know who made the door, but it's thicker and sturdier than I thought. The bullet didn't do anything against it. I could fire more rounds at it, but I don't think it would be worth it. I better save these bullets for something more important."

Like someone here trying to kill me, which was possible, especially given that Danilo was here and his men were probably searching for him. When all hell broke loose here, I would need protection against them.

"Really?" He asked, stepping to the door and then stopping behind it. He checked the doorknob to make sure that I was telling him the truth and then groaned when he found out that I wasn't lying. "You're entirely right about it. Whoever built this house, they really knew what they were doing."

And then I heard another pair of footsteps coming this way, and I wasn't surprised when I saw none other than Ferlisha and Danilo. I was already disappointed that she looked all sweaty and tired, which meant that they were having sex before I fired the gun, which was to be expected.

"What happened?" Danilo asked, panting slightly. He ran all the way here from the room where he was, which was the first thing that caught the attention of my eyes. I knew that he had already picked one of the rooms, but I didn't think that it was so far away from here. It was something that I was going to keep in mind.

"He found a gun," Lester explained, pointing to it with his finger.

"So, he did," Danilo said, tipping up his chin as if he needed to show me he wasn't afraid of it. But it was a ground-breaking change and he was aware of that. So much so I was pretty sure he was making plans in his mind so that he could get the gun for himself, even though that was never going to happen.

"You're going to do anything against us with it?" Ferlisha asked, looking alarmed and making me think a thousand times about what my next action should be. I didn't want to startle her more than she already was and I wasn't going to.

I lowered my arm and tucked my gun into my waist, shaking my head.

"You don't need to worry about anything."

A moment of silence and we didn't know what to say. The fact that I had a gun now was game-changing and everyone was aware of that.

"That's good," Ferlisha said, stepping toward me, which was something that I was surprised about. I didn't think she was going to move away from Danilo and then to me, but she was doing that. Maybe she was thinking that, because I had a gun, I was the one she should be with, but I wasn't holding my breath for that.

After all, the two of them already had her and, as far as I was concerned, I couldn't be her fiancé and it would never change.

"I want to be close to you now," she explained and Danilo and Lester went tense. I figured she was going to say something groundbreaking, but I didn't think it was going to be that. I didn't think she was going to come with me.

"I can't let you do that," Lester said, throwing his arms over his head and looking disappointed and irritated. It wasn't that he had anything he could do about it, but that he thought she was going to be more loyal to him. And even I was being a lot more cautious than I would otherwise be because I was wary of what her intentions were.

I knew that Danilo and Lester already had her, that they were between her legs, and if she was my fiancée, then that was something hard to swallow. So much so that Ferlisha already looked disappointed that I wasn't falling head over heels for her.

"And neither can I," Danilo said, keeping his expression stern and as if he was going to attack me if I didn't do what he wanted. But what did he want that he could achieve? I asked myself. If Ferlisha wanted to spend the next couple of hours with me, then there was nothing they could do about that.

A moment of silence hung in the air and I couldn't do anything about it. I was tense. It was the first time that I was so tense in my life and I knew I couldn't stop feeling that way right now. So much so that my hand was already going for the pistol and, if I needed to use it, then I would.

I sighed, stepping away from them and Ferlisha looked lost, looking left and right as if she was wondering if they were going to say anything else. They were waiting for her answer, and when they found out that it wasn't the one they were looking for, they were disappointed.

Ferlisha went after me and I didn't look at her. Even though I was beginning to feel something strong for her – and I couldn't call it love – I also couldn't be with someone that already was with two other guys.

"What do you want?" I hissed, looking down at her for no more than a moment before stopping in front of the door of my room. If she was thinking she was going to get in with me, then she was going to be disappointed.

"Running away from me is pointless. I know that someone is monitoring what is happening here and if I don't find out who my fiancé is, then we'll be locked in this place forever."

"That's not going to happen. I'm going to make sure of it."

"You don't know that. You don't know what's going to happen here."

"I always make sure that I don't leave anything to chance," I explained, opening the door and then entering the room. I was closing the door when she put her hand against it, stopping me.

I shook my head as I put myself in the doorway so that she couldn't step inside.

"What do you think you're doing?" I asked and when I thought she was going to answer me or do something stupid, she pulled her hand from behind her back and showed me a piece of paper. Ever since finding that first note, I wondered if we were going to find something else, and so far I was disappointed that we didn't.

I made my eyes look more serious as I snatched the piece of paper from her hand.

"Come inside, and not a peep."

CHAPTER 10

Ferlisha

I imagined that showing that piece of paper to him was going to make him more malleable, and I wasn't surprised when I found out that it worked. He almost shoved me into his room, shut the door in a heartbeat with the key, and then turned to me as he stared at me with burning eyes.

He was scaring me, but I'd been in worse situations before in my life. And one of them was when we first met in the main hall.

"When did you find it?" He asked and his voice sounded so threatening I was worried I was going to piss myself. But thankfully, it didn't happen. I had no idea what I was even doing in his room. All I knew was that I needed to be here. It was the only way to find out more about him. I knew that Lester was a politician and Danilo was a mafia don, but this guy in front of me… He was a mystery.

"It was in Danilo's room…" I replied and he groaned, shaking his head.

"I figured that he was hiding something from me – as he should be – but I didn't think it was something so important."

"He's always going to be hiding something from us."

He smiled shyly and it didn't look good, and it couldn't be different. I supposed that smiling was something that he didn't do often, regardless of what was happening.

"You learn quickly, and it's a surprise. Being around us doesn't phase you."

"Maybe you're right, but I just wanted to make sure that you know about this, too. I know it doesn't make any sense, but if whoever put us in here wants us to do that, then I don't think there is much we can do about it."

"And what is it that he wants us to do?" He asked, opening the note and reading it. His hands were calm as he did that, most likely because nothing could phase him easily, and I appreciated that about him.

"This must be some kind of joke," he said through his breath, almost like he was trying to hide those words from me.

"I don't know anything about that, but I think we just have to do it."

He took a deep breath and then let it out through his mouth, looking a lot more stressed than I thought he could be. "He wants us to reenact the wedding."

"I was actually hoping I could learn a little more about you," I explained, and I wasn't surprised when he lifted his eyelids, staring at me. He was trying to read what I was thinking and it wasn't hard to do so.

"What do you want to know about me?"

"Like what you do for a living."

"Like what I do for a living?" He said, crumpling the piece of paper in his hand and then tossing it under his bed. Lester didn't know anything about it and I was going to have to tell him, which wasn't something I was looking forward to.

I nodded. "I know what Danilo and Lester do, but not you. You are a mystery, and I also know that you have to be feeling something strong for me, given that you are here with us."

"I don't think you need to know anything about that. It won't make a difference."

"That's where you're wrong. Without knowing that, I can't even find out if you are my fiancé or not. Remember that I was getting married before all this happened."

He groaned slightly, stepping away from me and then going to the window, looking outside. Iov appeared to be pensive, like he always was. He was always like that.

"What are you thinking?" I asked and I had no idea if he was even going to answer that. All I knew was that he was going to do what needed to be done to get out of here, whatever that was.

"It's late and I want to sleep. You should go back to your room."

"I don't want to go there."

"Why not?" He asked, not looking at me. He was just looking ahead and through the glass of the window, most likely making plans in his mind. Especially now that he had a gun, he could do whatever he wanted, including killing me.

Even though I didn't want to admit it, it was most likely one of the reasons why I was clinging to him now.

"Danilo and Lester could come looking for me and I don't want to talk to them."

"Regardless, you should leave. You aren't going to be feeling better staying here in my room. Not to mention that it isn't helping you remember anything."

I bit my bottom lip. Iov was so different from the other ones. I knew that he was trying to pretend he didn't care about me, but I was also aware that things were different.

He let me into his room because he wanted me close by. He was a little shy, but I was used to that. I knew what shy men were like, thanks to having a little brother that never felt like leaving his room.

"I'm going to sleep on the floor, then," I affirmed and it wasn't something that I was going to back down from. No matter what Iov said, he wasn't going to change my mind.

He groaned, shaking his head.

Iov didn't say anything, just proceeding to the bathroom, opening and then closing the door, and leaving me alone. I figured that he was going to do something like that, but I didn't think it was going to hit me so hard.

I didn't know why I was insisting on what I was doing, especially when it was obvious that he wasn't going to change his mind. When Iov wanted to be this way, he could be so stubborn.

I sat on the bed, closed my eyes, and then waited until he was done with his shower. I wasn't surprised when he stepped out of the bathroom, finding me and stopping in front of the doorway.

And I also wasn't surprised when he didn't say anything, even though I was disappointed that he already had his clothes back on and I wasn't able to see what he was like naked. I was curious. I'd already seen what Lester and Danilo were like without their clothes on, but not Iov, and even though it was something dirty and that made me feel filthy, it was still something that I couldn't get rid of.

"I don't know what you are still doing here. If you want to sleep on the floor, that's fine by me."

"I don't think that's true. You are lying to yourself and you are trying to lie to me, but it's not working."

He shook his head, waving his hand as he said, "I need to sleep. If you want to sleep on the floor, then do it. It's not going to make me change my mind."

Now I was beginning to feel irritated. I didn't want to sleep in my room because I was pretty sure I was going to be alone there and with my thoughts, and I had far too many of them right now. I was certain that neither Lester nor Danilo was going to come looking for me and that I was going to be so scared because I was going to be alone.

And yet, I couldn't imagine myself spending more than one night with someone that didn't even want to tell me what he did for a living. So why did I feel this attraction to him that was more than physical?

I was frustrated. I was frustrated because I didn't even know what was going on in my mind at the moment.

"Then, make the arrangements for the make-up wedding and

make sure that your vows are good enough, or else I might think that you aren't my fiancé even though you might be, and that would be a pity. I don't want to imagine what would happen if whoever is monitoring us finds out that I made the wrong choice."

"I think you should stop worrying about him and focus more on yourself," Iov said, opening the door for me and waiting until I stepped out of the room. When I was out of it, he shut the door behind me decisively, which really showed how much different from Danilo and Lester he was.

I was going to be in my room, alone, and it was going to be like torture.

CHAPTER 11

Ferlisha

"This is so fucking stupid," Lester said, trying to look a little more serious than his normal self. He looped his arm around mine and I could tell that he really didn't want to be doing this. He wanted to be doing something else, which was being on the platform in the little chapel that was in the mansion. And yet, we decided that Iov should be the one there.

Or maybe I should be saying that I was the one who made that decision, and mostly because I wanted to punish him for treating me the way he did last night. Last night was horrible, and he left me alone with my thoughts in my room, and I could never forgive him for that, even if he happened to be my fiancé.

"I know it is, but just play along."

We were in the doorway of the chapel, trying to reenact the marriage. Rows of benches lined up against the aisle, and on one of the two front benches was Danilo, who was seated there, and he looked like he didn't know what to be doing with his hands.

He wasn't even looking at me. He was disappointed that he also wasn't the one that was on the platform. Maybe he was thinking that I was already remembering that he wasn't my fiancé, but the truth was that I just didn't remember that. I still had no idea what happened before getting kidnapped.

"So, can you finally remember anything about what happened?" Lester asked, making me look up and I could remember that someone took me to where Iov was, but I couldn't remember if that was my father or someone else. I still had no idea why these three men were paired with me, and yet here we were.

I wasn't going to deny the fact that I was wanted by three men was exciting, though. It really was and I was milking it.

I shook my head. I noticed that Danilo was standing up and going to the platform on the other side of the chapel. He climbed onto it, went behind the main pillar, and then got from it what appeared to be a thick and long book. I didn't even know that it was there, but what he was doing made sense. Someone needed to be performing that part of the wedding.

"What?" He said, shaking his head. "Someone needs to be the priest."

"Is the music system ready to be played?" I asked, raising my voice and feeling something strange in my stomach. It wasn't that I was beginning to have a stomachache, but that it was like there was a knot in there that I couldn't do anything about. It was tight and was beginning to overwhelm me, but I was still ignoring it.

I could feel it because I was starting to remember what happened at the church during the wedding. I didn't think I was going to, but I was. Reenacting the marriage was going to make me remember some things, and many of them were some of the ones I didn't like.

"Yes, it is," Danilo said, pressing the button and when that classical wedding song started to play, I felt like everything around me was changing. I felt like I wasn't in a dark, foreboding chapel that didn't look inviting at all. I felt like I was back at the church and at the wedding, where I was going to get married to…

I suddenly thought I could remember his face, but it was still a blur. So much so that I tried not to focus too much on it. I could remember everything, I reassured myself.

We started to walk down the aisle and in less than a minute I was by the front of the raised platform, where Iov was waiting for me.

He wasn't smiling, as usual. He was looking pretty serious and almost like he was planning different ways to kill us, even though I was certain he wasn't going to do that. Not right now, anyway.

The wedding song stopped, and it still felt so surreal everything that was happening here. Danilo was the one holding the bible, Iov was pretending to be my fiancé, and Lester was the one delivering me. I felt like everything was happening in slow motion and too fast at the same time.

I could remember that my husband was on the platform at the real wedding, but I still couldn't remember his face. All I knew was that he was one of these men, and that they were all lusting after me.

"Remember that if you can't remember anything about this, then this is all pointless," Danilo said, looking at me while he still held the Bible in his hands. He was looking like a proper priest, which was unlike him. I never thought that he could look anything different from his mafioso persona.

"I am remembering some things," I explained, adding, "I can remember that this really happened before, but it's still a mystery to me who was chosen to be my husband. All I know is that he wasn't happy about the way this was happening."

"I wonder why," Lester grumbled, giving me to Iov even though it was obvious he didn't want to do that. If anything, I knew that he wanted to be kissing me and making love with me right in the chapel, even though he shouldn't even be thinking that.

"What do you mean?" I asked and he waved his hand, making me shut my mouth when I thought about insisting on that. I was going to ask him further questions about that, but it was obvious he wouldn't have answered them anyway.

"Nothing."

I shook my head. I really couldn't imagine myself getting married to someone like Lester, which was making me think that he didn't have anything to do with this. If anything, he had to be the one that locked us up in here and then gave us all amnesia.

I was with Iov and he was right in front of me, looking at me with his same stern and composed expression. It really was so difficult to be in his presence, which was making me imagine that he also couldn't be my fiancé. I just couldn't imagine myself spending the rest of my life with someone so dangerous and unfriendly.

Danilo breathed long and loudly, wishing that he was the one pretending to be my fiancé. He was holding the Bible in his hands when he opened it, looking for the right page. He was flipping through the pages when Lester noticed that he wasn't finding the one he was looking for, and so he went there to help him.

"It should be this one," he said, pointing at the page with his finger, which made Danilo groan as he probably thought that he looked a little stupid. But he didn't. If anything, he looked so cute that way. I never thought he could look cute.

Everything was so quiet around us that we could only hear, although only faintly, the howling wind outside. The candelabrum was the only thing illuminating the place, casting harsh shadows on it.

"Still nothing?" Iov asked, snapping my attention back to him.

I shook my head. "Nothing. This is more difficult than I thought, especially because I never thought I would have to be doing something like this."

And when this was over, I would have so many stories about this moment and this place to my family. They wouldn't believe any of it. I wondered what would happen when they found out who my fiancé was.

It was pretty obvious that they both wanted me and that I was beginning to feel something strong for them, even though I couldn't call it love.

"Well, this is pointless, then," Danilo said, looking like he was going to close the Bible, but then realizing that he shouldn't. After all, if he wanted to get out of here and he did want that, then he needed to go through with it. He needed to finish the whole thing.

"It's not. This is going to work and I'm pretty sure that whoever is monitoring us right now, even though we can't see any cameras, knows that we are doing this according to the way he wants."

"Maybe you're right," Danilo said, sighing again and then beginning to read what was on the page.

Lester was seated on the bench in front of us, his hands clasped in his lap. He was looking so lost, his eyes always on me as he showed me that he was the one that should be unofficially getting married to me.

And yet, the more this was going on, the more I was beginning to suspect that he couldn't be the one chosen to be my husband.

This would all be so much easier if only I could ask my father what needed to be asked, I thought.

And at least, I was getting married to Iov, even if only unofficially. He was looking intently at me and I knew that several things were going on in his mind. I wished I could see a fraction of them so that I could better understand him.

And the next thing, I was already thinking, we were going to do was our wedding night. We didn't have sex like I did with Lester and Danilo, but I was pretty sure that the thought was already in his mind and that he was craving it.

To be honest, I was excited. I knew that the feeling I was having was dirty and that it was making me feel filthy, but I still couldn't brush it off.

I was just… so excited and a little happy since this all started.

CHAPTER 12

Iov

"We shouldn't really have to do this. It doesn't make any sense and I'm pretty sure that Danilo and Lester are hating that we are doing it," I grumbled, opening the door of my room and letting her step inside. I couldn't do anything about it, given that I knew that whoever was keeping us locked in here was monitoring everything we were doing, including this.

So much so that he gave us another note saying that he was happy about the way we faked the marriage. He was content with that and now, to further appease him, I needed to have my wedding night with Ferlisha. Looking at her face, I knew she was enjoying this… And probably much more so than she should be.

"I knew you were going to cave in eventually," she said, closing the door behind her and then putting her weight against it, almost like she was trying to show me that she wasn't going to change her mind about it.

And fuck, was she stunning and I couldn't oppose her proposal for much longer. From head to toe, one of the most beautiful women I'd seen in my life and that was putting it mildly.

My dick was already getting hard at the thought of fucking her, even though I shouldn't. Even if I was supposed to become her real husband after this was all over, I didn't know if I wanted to be with her. And yet, my feelings for her just kept on getting stronger.

"And you still don't remember anything? You really don't remember who your real fiancé is supposed to be?" I asked and she shook her head, smiling gently. It was almost like she didn't want this to end, even though she should be.

After all, she was the one still wearing that wedding dress and it looked disgustingly filthy. And I still wanted to rip it off of her as quickly as possible so that I could see how stunning her body was without it.

She shook her head and then responded, "No, I don't and I don't think that this is really helping. Even though I see some flashes of what happened before, I don't think they are relevant. I think that whoever is behind this is just playing with us."

I shook my head, finding all this unbelievable. Maybe Ferlisha was right about it, but I wasn't in my right state of mind to be thinking about that right now. At the moment, the only thing I wanted to be thinking about was letting out some of the stress.

After all, I had to be on my toes all the time, especially when I was next to Lester and Danilo. They were both planning on killing me and now that I was the one with the gun, I was pretty sure they were even more assertive about that.

"Something going on that I should know about?" Ferlisha asked, stepping toward me and then grabbing my tie. I tried to move her hand away, but I couldn't deny that the way she was doing that was making me feel something for her I never thought possible. I never thought it was a part of me.

"No, nothing, and you should leave my room as soon as possible. Whatever you think you're doing, I know it's pointless."

"I don't think that's the case. Not to mention that we are supposed to be doing this. We need to have our wedding night or else whoever is behind this will keep us locked in here for the rest of our lives."

"I don't think so. Danilo's men are looking for him and they are bound to find us eventually."

"And do you think that can happen before it's too late and we run out of food?" She asked, finishing removing my tie and then putting it on top of the nightstand.

Everything was so quiet around us that I could almost hear a pin dropping. I could even hear her breathing, and it was slow and what I thought it sounded like. I could see the way her lips moved, the way her pupils were looking at me, and those things, alongside everything else, were turning me on so much I never thought it was possible to feel this way.

"I don't know, but I'm not waiting for anything," I said, trying to move away from her, but knowing that she wasn't going to have that. It was for that reason I wasn't surprised when I felt her hand grabbing mine, stopping me where I was.

"I feel something strong for you and I know you feel the same way," she said and I knew it had to be a lie. So much so that my eyes alone were showing that it wasn't going to change my mind. It wasn't going to make me think that I really could be her fiancé.

"I don't."

"Stop lying to me and you are going to be a much better person, and feel much better about yourself," she said and I knew it was true, at least in part. Not to mention that I could feel my orgasm showing up in me and making me feel much more lust for her than I ever thought possible.

I was already thinking about pleasing her in all the ways I could and I knew she was thinking the same thing.

"We should do this," she said, moving her hands between the gap of the black coat, opening it, and then taking it off me. And the most striking thing about that? It was that I was letting her do it, and there was nothing I could do to stop her. I wanted her to undress me, to finally feel a little less tense than normal.

"I don't think we should. I'm not your husband, Lester and Danilo could be your fiancé, and nothing is going to change that, unless you magically start remembering everything."

"You're like a broken record and I don't like that. It's one of the reasons why I'm getting so frustrated with you," she said, undoing the buttons of my office shirt and making me feel more exposed than I ever felt in my life, and I knew that it was supposed to be this way.

She took off my shirt, her eyes going up and down as she checked me out. She was loving what she was seeing, which was making me think that I should just give in to the avalanche of lust in my mind.

I was lusting after Ferlisha so hard I couldn't help but imagine what it would be like to grab her thighs with my hands, lifting her so that she put her legs around me, and then feel her pussy rubbing against my cock.

It had been a long time since I last had sex, which was something I wasn't proud of. If anything, I was beginning to think I should start to make up for the lost time.

"Are we going to do this, then?" She asked, going on her toes as she tried to kiss me and I knew that it was pointless to try to stop her, so much so that I didn't do that, just letting her lips connect to mine and it was like fireworks were set off in my mind.

Never before did I feel so happy and never before did I feel like no one was going to come after my life, even though I knew that it wasn't the truth. There was always going to be someone coming after me, especially given that I was part of the Walter Group.

When I broke the kiss, I said, "You are going to regret this. You don't know what I can do when I'm pissed," I growled, moving against her and putting my hands under her dress. She helped me lift it and then over her head, and in no moment at all, she was without it.

Her body was stunning without that wedding dress, which was just the way I thought it was like. Curvy, a little on the chubby side, but still with so much for me to grab on that it was intoxicating. I could imagine my hands sliding over her curves and I knew that I didn't have to be wondering what that was going to feel like.

It had to happen now and it was going to.

"Maybe. Are you finally going to tell me what it is that you do for a living?"

"Depends. Is that going to make you remember who your fiancé is supposed to be?" I hissed, moving my hand on her cheek and feeling it, enjoying how soft and warm it was. I was pretty sure she loved having my hand moving on her cheek, which was one of the reasons why she was looking so easy right now. She was begging for me to fuck her, and my prick was so hard to make that happen. I couldn't resist the urges that were sprouting in my body.

"It just might," she said, letting me move my arms around her body and find the snap of her bra. I dealt with it and she let the piece fall to the floor. When her boobs were free and looking perky, I couldn't help but feel my mouth salivating. It was the first time I was feeling something like that happen, and I wasn't ashamed of it. It was also the first time that I was in the presence of a woman so stunning.

"I don't know what it is you think you're doing, but it's working," I said, pushing her against the wall softly and then kissing her again, and then the sides of her neck, moving down to her breasts. I cupped them, kneading and massaging them, and she followed that with her moans. Ferlisha was enjoying it much more than she should be.

Lester and Danilo were going to be so pissed when they found out about what happened tonight. But it wasn't like they didn't have a clue, right? After all, this was supposed to be our wedding night and nothing was going to change that.

"Love hearing that from you, Iov," she said, that being one of the few times she said my name. I knew she would say it tonight, but it still felt odd hearing it coming out of her mouth.

My dick was hard and raging in my pants. And, fuck all this waiting and foreplay were torturing me. Whoever was keeping us locked in here wanted to see everything between us and he probably had some cameras set up in here too.

In that case, he could keep on spying on us and I was going to show him how to properly make love to a woman. If he was thinking that him watching this was going to dissuade me and make me think that I couldn't have some fun with Ferlisha, he had something coming. Not to mention that I was going to end his life when we met, too.

I was so sure of that my heart was burning in rage just thinking about it.

"Oh god, this is too much," Ferlisha moaned into my mouth. I kissed her again, loving her lips rubbing against mine, and I knew she was enjoying that as much as I was. This was far from over.

In fact, it was only starting.

CHAPTER 13

"You've been waiting for this moment to happen for a long time, haven't you?" Iov hissed into my ear, nibbling on my earlobe and making me wonder if he was already going to fuck me with his dick, and then making me feel a little surprised when he didn't. It was more than obvious that he was taking his time and I, in turn, was getting a little frustrated at that.

I lied down on the bed, waiting for him to do whatever he wanted to do to me. His eyes scanned me, checking me out and dissecting me with them.

"I knew you were stunning, but I didn't think it was like this. I didn't think you were so beautiful."

Was I allowed to be a little filthy right now? Hell yeah, I was, I thought, moving my finger up and down, from his head to his toe, making Iov question what exactly I meant by that.

"Take off your clothes and then you can remove my panties," I said and it surprised him, I noticed. But then his hands immediately went for the hem of his shirt and he took it off, showing me his jaw-dropping chest.

If I thought that Danilo had a whole collection of tattoos on his body, then Iov was in a league of his own. His body was covered by his tattoos, almost like he was born with them, even though it didn't make much sense. It didn't make *any* sense, I corrected myself.

Now that he was shirtless, his muscles rippling under the light coming from the lamps hanging from the walls, I couldn't help but notice that he looked like a God.

And that, in turn, made me crawl away from him, which was something I thought I would never do in the presence of a man. He was *that* scary. He was much scarier than Danilo and Lester, and that was saying something. They were both frightening in their own ways.

"I've been waiting for this," Iov murmured, climbing onto the bed and then quickly finding himself right on top of me. His lips were mere inches from kissing mine again, and I knew he was thinking about doing it. He was thinking about kissing me and my pussy was soiled, just wondering what he could do with his cock.

"You haven't taken off the rest of your clothes yet," I pointed out and that seemed to annoy him, though only a little. He groaned slightly, getting off the bed and then taking off his pants and his underwear, finally showing me how big his cock was.

I was more than impressed – it was paralyzing me where I was, and I knew that things were only going to get worse in that sense for me.

"Do you want to play with it?" He asked, climbing onto the bed again and when he was on top of me for the second time, I knew that there was nothing this time I could say that could change his mind. In other words, I poked the bear and he was angry at it. So much so that he was already thinking about doing unspeakable things to me.

I nodded, pursing my lips. I knew that I was almost making the wrong choice, but my body craved it. I craved having him inside of me, finally losing my virginity, and I knew that he was thinking the same thing.

"I want to do a lot more than that," I replied, grabbing his cock and then giving it a little squeeze. I didn't know how he was going to react to it, but I was surprised when I noticed him slightly closing his eyes and a moan escaping his lips.

It showed me that I was on the right track and that he was enjoying every moment of what was happening here so far. It gave me enough confidence to keep going and I was going to use that to my advantage.

I gave Iov's dick a couple of strokes, loving it, thinking that not even Danilo's felt like this. I was so sure of that I was already thinking that Iov just might be my fiancé, even though the implications of that were far too big for me to wrap my head around.

So much so that I didn't even want to think about them and the only thing that was populating my mind right now was showering myself with the pleasure that I was going to feel from this.

"You're looking a little shyer than I thought you were going to be," he murmured, kissing my neck and then my breast, his lips scratching against my nipple. And he did that slowly, as if to show me that he was only playing with me right now, which was certainly the case. I was so sure about that that I wasn't even wondering if something else was happening behind the scenes.

"I'm taking my time," I purred, putting my arms around him and then bringing him down against the bed, which was something I thought was going to be a lot more difficult to pull out. I was on top of him a moment later and he was welcoming it, smiling broadly. It was the first time I was seeing Iov smiling like this, and it was refreshing.

"I want this."

"Do you really want it, or are you just playing with me right now?" He asked and I knew that it wasn't a real question. I knew that because he dropped his hands on my ass, kneading and massaging the skin. I feared that he was looking for my asshole, and I wasn't surprised when he found it.

Giving it a couple of strokes, he brought me more pleasure than I thought possible, and I feared I was going to come hard and was going to pass out, but I was happy when it didn't happen. It meant that there was still so much more to happen here and that Iov was more than willing to be part of it.

"I want all of it."

"I don't feel conviction in the way you said that," he murmured, moving his hands over my thighs, letting me move down so that my mouth was no more than a couple of inches from his cock. My heart was beating like a jackhammer in my chest. It was the first time that I was so close to sucking off a dick and I was almost certain that Iov was thinking the same thing, too.

My lips were dry all of a sudden and I didn't even know what was happening to me anymore. I felt his hand suddenly looking for my hanging breast. He pressed his fingers against it, moving them around it, and just that was enough to make me feel that I was going to have the climax of my life. I was so certain it was going to happen I was already readying myself for it and I was a little disappointed when it didn't happen.

"Let me have a little taste of it," I murmured and I knew he wanted that.

I watched him as he pursed his lips and when he nodded, I knew I had the go-ahead. I was so certain of it I was already wrapping my lips around his massive dickhead, loving it, swirling my tongue around it, and then giving his balls a couple of squeezes.

They were massive and I didn't know if they were even bigger than Danilo's. Now that I was remembering what happened that night, I knew that we never reached this point in our sex, and that was a little disappointing.

Regardless, I wasn't going to be thinking about that sort of thing right now. The only thing that I wanted to be thinking about was giving Iov the most pleasure of my life, for I was beginning to remember something important, though it wasn't that he was my fiancé or anything of the sort.

I pulled my head back up at the same moment I noticed he was about to erupt, and then he did, shooting his come all over my face. The speed and the pressure with which it came out were surprising and I wasn't expecting it.

So much so that I began to blink uncontrollably, even though I soon got used to his viscous globs on my face. I even scooped some of his sperm with my fingers and licked them off.

That seemed to please him, and thus he wrapped his arms around me, pulling me down so that I was against his body.

Our night together was just beginning, and when I felt the warmth of his chest against my head, I remembered one more important thing, and this one was game-changing.

I didn't know how he was going to take it, but it needed to be said nonetheless.

CHAPTER 14

Danilo

I couldn't believe it, standing in the hole that was under me, noticing that I could finally – maybe – escape this place and find myself in a much better place where I didn't have to be thinking about the things that were happening in this mansion. And one of them was the fact that Ferlisha seemed to be remembering something she shouldn't.

I was hoping that she was going to say I was her fiancé, but the fact that she was spending much more time with Iov was telling me otherwise. It was telling me that she was in love with him and not me, which was hurting my heart more than I thought it ever would. It was doing much more than that, in fact.

It was destroying me from the inside out much more than it should, even making me think that I shouldn't tell her anything about this. I shouldn't tell Ferlisha about this hole in the ground that was going to lead me out of here.

I looked over my shoulder, hoping that nobody was suddenly going to enter my room and find me looking down at the floor. Everything around me, including the hallways that led to my room, was quiet. I could even hear my own breathing, which was something that didn't happen often.

I took a deep breath, readied myself to jump into the hole, and when I was going to do it, I heard knocks on the door. For a moment, I thought that I was only hearing things, that I was imagining it, but then I found out that it was indeed happening.

I stood up slowly, wondering what I should do right now. If someone was indeed on the other side of the door and wanted to talk to me, then I should do it. I should talk to that person, convince them that nothing important was going on in my room, and then get out of here before it was too late.

It had already been weeks since we were left in this mansion and I was pretty sure that my men were still looking for me. I just needed to walk around a bit on the premises until I stumbled into them.

I beelined to the door, stopping behind it and then looking through the spyhole. I blinked once and when I noticed the figure behind the door, I knew that it matched the knocks I heard before. It was Ferlisha and even though I thought it could also be someone else, I knew that her presence here was much more of a coincidence.

Even though she wasn't as dangerous as we were, she was always on the lookout for opportunities. So much so that she was probably smelling that something was up.

"Danilo, I hope you are in there because I need to talk to you," she said and I expected she was going to say that. She was gaining more confidence as time passed here and I knew that she was growing overconfident, especially because she was making us drool over her like we were nothing more than savages looking for our next catch.

Regardless, it wasn't like she was going to influence me right now. I was only a little annoyed that I needed to talk to her at the same moment when I was going to finally get out of this place. It was beginning to get into my head and make me have thoughts I never thought I would.

"Yeah, I'm here," I said, not showing any excitement in my voice, even though her presence here was making me feel the opposite. I knew that I wanted to be with her, that I wanted her in my arms again, but it was so difficult to think that when I knew she had been with Iov so many times before after our first night.

I felt that she was already taken, which wasn't something that I was going to be obsessing over. If Ferlisha was already taken, then there was nothing that could be done about it. Not to mention that I had better things to do, including finding my men and going back to my old life.

I opened the door and I found her in front of me, and she took a deep breath, trying to look over my shoulder even though she was too short for that.

"Are you hiding something, Danilo?" She asked, trying to get into the room, but I stopped her. I put myself in front of her and it was enough to deter her, though I didn't know for how much longer. When she was obsessed with something, she could always do it.

"No, I'm not. I hope you didn't come here just to ask me that," I said, hoping that she was just going to leave me alone, but when it became obvious that she wasn't, I couldn't help but groan.

"No, I came here because I need to tell you something. It's pretty important."

The gleam in her eyes was telling. I knew she was getting ready to drop a bomb on me and I didn't know how I was going to take it. All I knew was that it was going to be massive and that it was going to leave me flabbergasted.

"What is it?"

"Can I go in so that we can sit and talk about it?" She asked, biting her bottom lip and I knew that it was a trap. Everything she wanted was to find out what I was hiding from her, given that she knew something was indeed amiss with me.

"No, you can't do that. I thought we had something special between us, but now I realize you were just toying with me."

"What do you mean?" She asked, trying to step into the room again, but I stopped her one more time. I was going to impede her from finding out about the hole in the ground as many times as needed.

"You were spending more time with Iov than you should," I explained and I hated that I was putting myself in this humiliating position where I was showing this weakness of mine. Someone my age, already over 35, should already be settled with a pretty, stunning woman, but it was the opposite that was happening. I just couldn't find someone I was happy with, and I didn't think that would change anytime soon.

"I was actually thinking that he really isn't the right person for me," she said, stepping away from me after dropping that bomb, and then I grabbed her hand before she could go anywhere.

"What do you mean?" I hissed, pulling her to me and when she lost her balance and fell into my arms, I knew that she was probably planning this as well.

She was always so sly it was unbelievable.

"I mean that I don't think he is my fiancé, or was it. I think that it might be you."

I widened my eyes. The time that we were spending here in this mansion was allowing me to get closer to her, to get to know her better, but I still thought that it wasn't love. But now that she was saying that, I was beginning to suspect it might be.

And if she was in love with me, then everything made sense. It meant that I was also in love with her, even though I always said that it was nothing more than just strong feelings that began to sprout in my mind.

"Did he hurt you?" I asked, feeling more protective of her all of a sudden. I didn't think I was ever going to feel this way about her, especially after we met for the first time in the main hall, but things were different now.

After getting to know Ferlisha so much better, to know what she was like, I knew we could be perfect together, if only we weren't stuck in this mansion.

She shook her head. "He can't. I know he never would hurt me, but it still doesn't mean that I want to be with him. I don't want to be with him because he's always so cold, always so distant from me, and always brooding and so introspective. Sometimes, I need something else. Sometimes, I need someone else, and I think that someone else might be you."

Her eyes were staring into mine and I knew that it meant so many things I just couldn't pretend that this wasn't happening. All I knew was that I needed to have her, to have her in my arms much more strongly than it was happening now, and so I made a choice.

I didn't know if it was the right one, but it was the only one that I could make at this moment.

And even though it meant that I was probably making more enemies than I ever did in my life, I felt right doing it.

I shut the door behind me and I knew that we were going to escape this mansion together.

CHAPTER 15

Ferlisha

When I opened my eyes and found myself in his room, I knew that something was up. And when my eyes diverted to the right and I found the hole in the ground, I knew that this was the moment I was looking for. I couldn't believe it.

My body was suddenly frozen in place. There was this huge hole in the floor, and it must have appeared out of nowhere, even though that didn't make much sense. If it was made recently, then why didn't we hear any noise?

"What the hell?" I asked, moving out of his arms and then toward the hole, stopping in front of it as I tried to make sense of this.

"I know that we scoured this place as much as we could, but I ended up stumbling into this and I opened this secret passage when I thought that I was already beginning to give up. I know that it doesn't make much sense, but it's what happened."

I turned around, finding out that he was right in front of me and that the glint in his eyes was telling me something else. Danilo was right about what he said. He wasn't lying about it, but he was still conflicted about something, and I wanted to find everything about it.

"So, you just stumbled into this hole in the floor, and you

weren't going to tell me anything about it?" I asked, finding the whole notion of that happening unbelievable. I thought that we were together when it came to getting out of this hellhole, but it appeared that he had other plans in mind and that they didn't necessarily include me. Not until now.

"Do you believe me?" Danilo asked, taking another step toward me and then putting his hand on my waist, bringing me closer to him and making me wonder if he was going to kiss me now.

I wanted to feel his lips again, but that was so difficult when I was beginning to get a little confused about my feelings as well.

After all, I was beginning to feel something for Lester and Iov too, even though the latter was still his usual self and I didn't think that anything in that sense was going to change. He was always going to be distant, introspective, and always thinking about himself only, even though sometimes he also remembered that I existed.

"I do," I said, our lips brushing again, but it was only momentarily. I didn't know if we could ever kiss so strongly, so passionately like before after finding out that he was hiding this from me. Danilo was hiding the way out of this mansion for himself and I didn't think I could forgive him for that.

"And yet, it appears that you are hiding one more thing from me," he said, locking his eyes with me, and I could feel the warmth of his body bathing me in it, making me want more of him, and I didn't know if I should do it with him right now.

The door was locked with the key, nobody was going to come in, and everything was fine even if we had sex, but there was still the problem that I didn't want Iov and Lester to find out that we did it. After all, they were gunning for me as much as this man was.

"We should leave this place as soon as possible. If I'm hiding something from you, then when we are out, I can tell you everything," I proposed and he groaned. It was obvious that he didn't like it, that he wanted me to tell the truth right at this moment, but things weren't so easy. I knew I couldn't trust Danilo entirely, but I still thought that we had something important going on between us.

"I don't like it, but you are right. Promise me this one thing," he said, cupping my cheeks with his hands and staring into my eyes. It was almost like he was trying to read what I was thinking, but it wasn't going to be so easy. It was much harder when it came to doing that, I thought, even though it wasn't necessarily true. All I knew was that I was going to make it harder for him than it normally was. "You shouldn't tell them about this. Let's leave this place as soon as possible and then, when you are living with me, you can tell me if you remember anything and if I'm your fiancé. Even if I'm not, then what does it matter? The truth is that I feel something strong for you and I want to find out more about it."

I looked over his shoulder and at the door that was behind him, and I just couldn't do what he was asking me to do. When it came down to it, I was also beginning to feel something strong for Iov and Lester, and I didn't want to cut my ties with them. So much so that I sighed, looking away from his eyes.

"I don't think I can do that," I said, looking down and then at my feet. If there was one other thing I wanted to be doing right now, it was buying new shoes so that I could walk without hurting my feet. Not only was the floor of this mansion not up to scratch, but the sandals that I wore also weren't helping, either. They weren't made for me to be walking on this wooden floor, which was one of the reasons why I hated that they put me in this mansion. It was so old it made me wonder why it was still here. Whoever owned it, he should have already destroyed it and built something better here.

He sighed, looking at the door and then moving away from me. I tried to grab him again, but it was pointless. He went to the hole in the floor, I thought that he was going to jump into it, but when it was obvious that he wasn't – not without me - I was a little more relieved, even though it wasn't enough.

"If you can't come alone with me, then this is pointless. I need to go back to my men, they are waiting for me, and you can come with me as well, but only if you are alone. Iov and Lester… I'm not going to take them with me, especially given that Iov has a gun and he could kill both of us easily, and nobody would ever find out the truth."

I took a deep breath in, but I wasn't going to do what he wanted. So much so that I was already going to the door, I opened it, and then I stepped into the hallway.

I feared I was going to have to search in the mansion for the guys, but then when it was obvious that they were already coming looking after me in the hallway, I was relieved. I was so relieved that I smiled, even though that wasn't something I was doing often here.

And I knew that I was betraying Danilo, but there was also no other way around it. He wanted to get out of here and we were going to, even though I was still not exactly sure who was supposed to be my fiancé.

I was beginning to think that it was that way because I might have been in love with all of them before this, and I didn't know if I was. It was a little suspicion that was sprouting in my mind and I couldn't do anything about it.

All I knew was that I was far too curious and far too determined to find out who my husband was supposed to be. So much so that I was waving my arms over my head and waiting for them to come, which they did in a heartbeat.

And when they were with me, the gleam in their eyes told me that they were worried about what I had to say.

Danilo was going to be angry and disappointed with me, but there was nothing that he could do about it. All I was thinking about at the moment was getting out of here as soon as possible.

And with all of them.

CHAPTER 16

Lester

This was unbelievable, but it was happening. I was with Iov, Danilo, and Ferlisha, and we were all in the same hotel room. We finally escaped that mansion even though Ferlisha still didn't know who her fiancé was. I was beginning to think that something else was at play here, but I didn't say anything about it. Not right now, anyway.

I was seated on a chair, my hands clasped in my lap and looking from left to right, checking out Ferlisha and the guys, too. We were all in the same room and there was this huge, heated discussion going on.

Ferlisha wanted to be with all of us at the same time and I just couldn't believe it. I was getting ready to call my advisors about where I was and tell them to come to pick me up. And after that, there would be a huge investigation into that mansion and they would find out who put me there, even though, until then, I knew that it was going to take a while.

I wasn't holding my breath for it. When it came to the police, they were always incompetent at their job. It was one of the things about them I wanted to change. I knew that it was going to take a while, but I was going to make it happen.

Everyone always thought that we politicians were always only worried about ourselves, but that wasn't the case. Not with me.

When people elected me, I made a promise to them. I promised that I was going to make the police better and, before I died, I was going to make that happen. I was going to make it real.

"But the truth is that I can't seem to remember what happened at my wedding and I… just want to be with all of you."

Ferlisha said that and everyone in the room was flabbergasted. I was only with them in the same room because she was important to me and I couldn't see myself going anywhere without first resolving this.

I wasn't going to tell the police about Iov and Lester, even though I should. I didn't want to put a bigger target on my head than there already was. It wasn't that I was afraid of them, but that I didn't think I wanted to mess with that right now.

I just wanted to find out if Ferlisha felt the same for me. I wanted to find out if she was as strongly in love with me as I was with her.

I stood up, noticing that whatever was going on here wasn't going to work. It wasn't going to make me figure out what was really happening. So much so that I was making a decision that was going to leave everyone surprised, and I knew that they thought the same.

They were even looking at me as everything fell silent in the room. I noticed that the bed was big enough for all of us. I thought that Ferlisha was going to order different rooms for all of us, but then she picked this one for all of us, and I could tell that meant she had something in her mind she wanted to tell us.

"It's pointless, anyway. I don't remember you before we met in that mansion, and this is going to lead nowhere. Let's just all get out of here and then go our separate ways," Danilo proposed, but he was also wrapped around her finger, and that meant he was going to do what she wanted, regardless of how ridiculous it was.

"It's not pointless, and you saying that hurts me," Ferlisha said, turning around and wrapping her torso with her arms, looking hurt.

Seeing that, I had to do something, which involved beelining to her and wrapping her shoulder with my arm. Danilo and Iov looked tense while seeing that, but there was nothing that they could do about it.

The discussion they were having really wasn't helping with anything, and everyone was aware of that. I could feel it exuding out of their eyes. The more time was passing, the more we wanted to do something about that, too.

"They are jerks. Come with me and I guarantee that you're going to have a much better life with me," I promised her and I knew she wanted to think about it, but she was still a little conflicted.

I didn't know why her mind was so difficult, but it was and I couldn't do anything about it.

She turned around, tears streaming down her cheeks, and, seeing that I just had to do the craziest thing. I kissed her, right in front of everyone, and I knew I was creating more dissent. So much so that Danilo ran up to me, punched me, and I jumped back up on my feet.

Iov didn't do anything, looking more composed, but I was still sure that he was still thinking that he should do something. He wasn't going to hurt me right now, but he would later. If he feared that I was going to steal his woman, then he wouldn't hesitate before slicing my neck with his wife.

Or shooting me in the back when I least expected it.

Anyway, kissing Ferlisha was worth it. Her lips were so delicious I just wanted to have more and more of them, and I knew she was thinking the same way.

She cupped her mouth with her hands, looking at me like she couldn't believe what was happening. It was the first time that we were resorting to violence, and things couldn't get much better from now on.

Danilo was huffing, his hand lifted and clenched, and I knew that he was thinking about extending this little quarrel between us. The only problem was that Ferlisha was now between us and she wasn't going to go anywhere. That was evident in the way she was staring at us.

"I think we can all agree that this is pointless and that you shouldn't be fighting," she said and the tears streaming down her face told me everything I needed to know. She was so much in love with us that she couldn't see us fighting. In fact, finding among ourselves was only hurting her and that was something that we could both agree on.

I lowered my arm, unclenching my hand. There was no point going any further with this if it meant that I was only hurting her. I didn't want to hurt Ferlisha more than she already was, especially because she had already gone through so much in that mansion.

"And I think I know who my fiancé is supposed to be," she said, turning her head from side to side as she looked at all of us, finally showing us that what we were doing wasn't for nothing.

"You gotta be kidding," I said, stepping toward her. "Then, you have the duty to tell us who he is. I won't settle for less."

"I know, but it's so difficult. I don't think I want you to know the truth."

"And what about the person that was monitoring us this whole time? Do you think he was the one that made that hole in the ground?"

"I don't know," Ferlisha said, shaking her head. "And I don't think that it matters anyway. What matters is that we are finally together, out of that mansion, and that you are with me. After learning who you are, I just want to say that you are everything to me. I love all of you equally and that's not going to change."

I took a deep breath in, stepping toward her and grabbing her hand. I could see that Ferlisha needed my support now more than anything and if that meant sharing her with Iov and Danilo, then so be it. I wasn't supposed to do it. I'd rather not do it, but there was no way around it.

"If it makes you happy, then I'm okay with it," I said and I could see her eyes gleaming with happiness. Never thought I would see her so happy, stepping outside the mansion, and I was witnessing that right now.

"Are you okay with this, too?" She asked Iov and Danilo, and the latter sighed and the first shook his head in disapproval, even though I could tell that they were both going to do what she wanted.

I was so sure of that I wasn't surprised when Iov stepped toward her. His eyes locked with me and I knew that he had several things to tell to me, but he was going to keep his mouth shut.

And one of the reasons for that was that he was aware that going up against me would hurt him more than it would accomplish anything.

His eyes met Ferlisha's and he said, "If it's going to make you happy, then I'm okay with it, too. No matter what happens, I'm going to stay by your side and I want to make you happy, even though that means spending time with someone I couldn't care less about."

I wasn't hurt by his words. I expected them, after all.

Now that he was okay with the direction our love was taking, that left only Danilo. He'd gone to the window and was looking outside and I had no idea what was going on in his mind. All I knew was that he was thinking about a lot of things, weighing his options.

He could go back to his old world, his life in the mafia, and pretend that nothing of this was happening, but it wouldn't really accomplish anything, especially because he was in love with her as well.

And knowing that being in love meant a lot of things and that not all of them were good, I was pretty sure that he could make only one choice.

He stepped back toward us, grabbed her hand, and I could see that his eyes were slightly watery, which was something I thought

I would never witness. It was making my heart a little tight. It was always so different when I was seeing someone going through something he wasn't used to.

"It's just as they said. If it makes you happy, then I'm okay with being your husband as well, though the fact that you are keeping the truth hidden from us is something that I'm not okay with."

She turned so that her eyes were solely focused on his. I could see that she was saying so much through the way she was looking at him and I knew that this moment meant more to her than anything else that ever happened in her life. Ferlisha was learning what true love was like, and it was eating her from the inside out, even though she knew it was the only thing she could do right now.

"Promise me one more thing."

"What do you want me to promise you?" Danilo asked, looking determined to do whatever she wanted. That was the thing about love. When only one thing was possible, when someone was deeply in love, they were always going to do whatever their pair wanted.

This was quite difficult for me as well, especially because it was the first time that I found myself in this situation. I was a little nervous and my heart was beating a little fast, but it was okay. I was with Ferlisha, we were finally choosing the path that made us happy, and it couldn't be any other way.

"Promise me that you won't try to find out the truth about the wedding, what I'm keeping hidden from you, and that you want to be with me as well. We can find a place big enough for the four of us, we can live in it, we can raise a family in it, and we can be happy."

He took a deep breath, but I knew that he was going to say what Ferlisha wanted. And thus, I wasn't surprised when he did.

"All right. I'm not going to look for anything and, even if I stumble into the truth, I'll keep it hidden. I think that's the least I should do and it's also the right thing."

And so, this was going to happen. I was going to be with Fer-lisha, Iov, and Danilo, all of us living under the same roof, and I never thought that my life was going to take such a turn.

CHAPTER 17

Ferlisha

We left that hotel and went back to the city, having not heard anything about who put us in that mansion, though everyone was looking into it and questioning as many people as they could, even though they were also doing everything in their power so that they didn't find out who I had chosen to be my fiancé. I feared, if they found out the truth, that it would destroy us and I wasn't looking forward to that.

Looking outside the new mansion where I now lived, I was just happy that I finally had a place where I didn't feel like I was in danger all the time. The place was big, spacious, and it even had a beautiful garden and a large swimming pool.

I always took some dives into it and spent some time there when I needed to get some of the stress out of my mind, and it was so great that I was already thinking about doing that a bit sooner than normal.

I knew that the guys were going to appreciate it, especially because they always said that I needed to be a little bit more relaxed when it came to enjoying myself. I was always paranoid, so doing that was a little bit more difficult than it was for most people.

Thinking that, I went to the door of the room, into the hallway, and then to the first floor of the mansion. On my way there, I greeted some of the employees and guards that worked for us.

They kept the place safe.

And if there was something that made this place a lot better than the mansion where I was locked with my husbands, it was the fact that it was modern and the floors weren't dusty and dirty all the time.

When I was outside, I closed my eyes and bathed in the warmth of the light of the sun, loving it. I then went to the swimming pool, took a shower under one of the showerheads close to it, and then jumped into the water graciously. The water was lukewarm and perfect for this hot Sunday.

I just got my head out of the water when I noticed that someone was also jumping into the water. None of the guards and none of the other employees would be doing that, so I wasn't surprised when I saw none other than Lester swimming toward me.

He was shirtless and with only his shorts and underwear on, his shoulder-length hair a little glued to his face and body thanks to it being wet.

"It's a beautiful day and I'm not surprised that I see you here now," he said, putting his arm around me, around my waist, and pulling me toward his body. Even though he was a politician and spent most of his time seated behind a desk, his body was well-built and he worked out often.

"I thought I was going to have some more private time." I pouted and I thought that he wasn't going to enjoy my little display of being genuine about something, but that was not what happened.

"Princess, in this house you can never have private time."

I could feel the warmth of his body, how his arm was making me feel protected, and I was loving how hard his muscles were.

I could feel them moving, shifting slightly, and it was everything needed to get me going. My sex was already getting a little wet and I was pretty sure that Lester loved that.

"Do you want to do something special?" I asked, wrapping my arms around his neck and then moving so that my boobs were pressing against his body, and I could see the gleam of lust in his eyes. It was everything I needed to know.

I knew that he was going to say yes, that he wanted to make love to me while we were still swimming in the pool, and that was exactly also what I wanted.

"And what is it that you want?"

"I don't think I should tell you that beforehand." I lowered my arm in the water, finding his groin and cupping it. I glanced at his lips as they parted, and I knew that was exactly what he was looking for when he came here and jumped into the water.

"You are always such a tease and trying to make me feel more pissed at you than I should be," he groaned and I knew that I had the go-ahead to sneak my hand under his flimsy shorts. And I did that, finding his cock and noticing that it was already hard. It couldn't be any different.

"We should do this before the others find out what's happening."

He widened his eyes slightly. "I knew you were going to say something that was going to make me ask why you are even doing this, but I didn't think it was going to be something so groundbreaking."

I pecked his lips, diving underwater before moving so that I was right in front of his groin. I lowered his shorts, licked my lips, and then opened my eyes until I could see that his dick was right in front of my face, and it looked so mean that it was difficult for me to wrap my head around what was unraveling in front of me.

And the only thing I couldn't stop thinking about was the fact that I was still a virgin. I should do something about that, even though it was going to take a while.

I thought that we were going to make love in that hotel room and that they were all going to take my V-card there at the same time, but everything then was still such a whirlwind that we didn't have enough time for it. And now, things were much different. Much, much more so.

And yes, I was being extremely dirty right now. I was always a filthy girl and that wasn't going to change.

"Well, the other guys aren't going to be happy about this," Lester groaned, but then he was quickly closing his eyes and letting me do everything I wanted to his white cock. It was massive, veiny, and it looked so mean that it was frightening me, though only a little.

If he was thinking that I was going to back away from this, then he had something coming.

I licked my lips, closed my eyes again, and then lowered my head until my lips were wrapped around his mushroom-like dickhead. I had watched some videos on YouTube on how to give proper blowjobs and I was already applying some of the tips I learned.

I was focusing the movements of my tongue on the underside of his dickhead and he was loving it. So much so that I could feel his legs trembling and looking a little more tense than normal. His legs were quite hairy and I loved that about him.

I started to please his legs, moving my hands over them, but when I realized that what I was doing wasn't enough, I cupped his balls with my right hand. I started to squeeze and tug at them slightly, noticing how warm they were.

His nuts were bigger than I imagined, and I couldn't wait until he was pounding in and out of me, slapping his ballsack against my ass, and the more time was passing here, the more I knew he was also thinking the same thing.

His dick was so big that it was almost overwhelming and I couldn't stop what I was doing anymore. I could feel that my pace was increasing, that I was getting more and more comfortable with the size of his slab of man meat, and everything was getting so sloppy and wet.

I knew that it was getting more and more difficult for me to continue the blowjob, but I still wasn't going to stop it. If there was something I wanted to taste for the first time, it was his come and

I was pretty sure that Lester thought the same way.

So much so that I wasn't surprised when I felt him grabbing my head with his hands, pushing it further down along the length of his prick, and then him pounding me until my mouth was sore. And the best thing about that? It was that this was just the beginning.

He pulled his hands back when he knew that he was close to erupting. He couldn't orgasm anywhere that wasn't in my mouth and thus I wasn't surprised when I started to feel his dick squirting his come inside of it, giving me that salty taste that I was looking for.

I swallowed everything and then when I felt that something else was in the water of the swimming pool, I knew that things had just begun.

CHAPTER 18

When I saw that Lester's head was over the level of the water, that someone else was under it, and that a woman was giving him a blowjob, I knew that she could be none other than Ferlisha.

I was a little irritated that this was happening without my knowledge about it, but there was nothing that could be done. Nothing that could fix it, I told myself. There were plenty of things that could remediate this developing situation, though.

At least, I wasn't alone. I was with Danilo and he also jumped into the water with me, following me. We went after Ferlisha and Lester and when we got to them, we didn't punch his greasy, mocking face, even though we should. Just like that other time we were in that hotel room, it wasn't worth it.

I just wanted to make sure that Ferlisha was having a good time and it appeared that I was being successful with that.

She emerged from underwater, shaking her head and then moving her hair so that it was behind her head. She opened her eyes and then fluttered her eyelids, though only momentarily.

When she realized that Danilo and I were here with her, she smiled. Her smile was always pretty, especially because she always went to the dentist when she needed to make her teeth look even whiter than they were.

"Hello, boys. Took you long enough. I knew you were going to come."

"I'm a little disappointed that you started this earlier than usual and without me," Danilo growled, glaring at Lester, even though he wasn't going to do anything against him. He was disappointed, but keeping Ferlisha happy was the most important thing to him, just like it was to me.

"I just couldn't stop myself. When I looked outside my window and I saw how the water was sparkling under the light of the sun, I just had to come here. I know you understand me."

"I do," I said, moving over to her, putting an arm around her, and thinking about doing unimaginable things to her boobs. I knew she wanted me to do that, but since she decided to commit this sin and suck off Lester without telling us anything about it, then I was going to do that a little bit later than normal.

"And I also don't like what was happening here one bit," Danilo groaned, trying to push me away from her, but that wasn't going to work.

I lowered my head as I considered kissing my wife, but then I pulled it back when I remembered that her lips were all over Lester's prick. Even though we were beginning to get along and he was a cool guy, especially when he wasn't in his politician persona, I wasn't going to do that.

I didn't want to feel his come on my lips was all I was saying.

I feared that what I did was going to hurt Ferlisha's feelings, but that's not what happened. In a moment, I noticed that her hand was already searching in the water for my dick, and I closed my eyes and groaned slightly when I felt her wrapping it around it, even through my shorts. She was loving it. She knew that I was thick and big, and I also noticed that there was something else she wanted to tell us.

Whatever it was, I knew that it was going to be groundbreaking.

I moved my hand over her cheek, asking, "What is that you

want to tell us?" I asked, noticing how small she felt in my arms. Lester was still dazed by the blowjob that she gave him and Danilo was looking more and more irritated, but he wasn't going to do anything.

He knew that, in a fair fight, he would lose against me and that I was always overprotective of Ferlisha. If he tried to stop what I was doing right now, even though I wouldn't fight against him, I would do something to make sure that he never made the same mistake.

"There's something that I have to say before this goes any further," she announced, looking at me, then at Danilo, and then at Lester. He came over so that he was no more than a couple of inches from us, and I knew that he wanted to have her in his arms. And yet, just like with Danilo, I wasn't going to let him do anything of the sort.

"What is it?" Danilo asked, sounding more serious than normal. Even though he was always like that, what he said showed me that this was one of the most important moments of his life.

"I am a virgin..." Ferlisha revealed and that was certainly something that I didn't think I was going to hear. I knew that she was hiding something pretty important from us, but I thought that it was something to do with whoever locked us in that mansion. And thinking of it, I was close to finding out who did that.

"What?" I asked, sounding more flabbergasted than I was irritated that she was woman enough to keep that hidden this whole time, even though it made sense that it was this way.

When it came down to it, her family was extremely religious and they always made a point that she had to remain pure so that her husband was the one to take her virginity after they consummated the wedding.

"It's true," she said, closing her eyes and I knew that whatever was happening here couldn't go on much longer, not without taking it outside of the water. There was this one thing that we wanted to do, that we had been planning on doing without her knowledge, and I knew that Ferlisha was going to love it.

I just never thought that it was going to happen as a way to show her how great having sex for the first time was.

"Well, that means we have to do something about that," Lester said, swimming over to us and, when our eyes locked, I knew what he was talking about.

And being aware of that, I pushed Ferlisha out of the water so that she was lying on the tiles of the floor around the swimming pool. She had a victorious smile on her face, knowing that we were going to finally take her virginity.

I grabbed her in my arms, lifting her up and taking her somewhere more private, even though that wasn't her bedroom, or our bedroom, to be more precise. It was a tiny little place we were building exactly for a similar purpose, though I never imagined that it was going to be to take her virginity.

She was still in my arms when I looked down, asking, "Are you ready for it?"

She nodded, pursing her lips. She was showing her nervousness and I knew that this was taking quite a toll on her, but she was going through with it no matter what.

I put her down on her bed, getting rid of her bikini in a heartbeat. It was only getting in the way and was quite annoying, I thought. Danilo and Lester were around the bed as well and they were just waiting for the action to start. They were so ready for it that they were already lowering their shorts and stepping out of them.

They were hard just looking at her lying on the bed, looking all exposed and vulnerable. And even though she was feeling like that, we weren't going to take advantage of her.

This was going to be a little competition between us, so that we could find out who, between us, could best please her.

When it came to Ferlisha, we were always very competitive and so this was just one more entry in the history of that.

I took a deep breath in, climbing onto the bed and then putting myself between her legs. I was already going to start wetting her pussy when I felt a hand settling on my shoulder.

I figured that it was Lester and I wasn't surprised when I looked over my shoulder, seeing his face and how stern he looked. It was the first time I was seeing him looking so serious.

"I don't think Ferlisha wants to know who is going to take her virginity when it happens," he growled and I knew that his mind couldn't be changed about it, nor Ferlisha's.

And it was for that reason that I was already crawling off the bed and then looking at Lester and Danilo. If this was going to happen that way, then Ferlisha needed to know about it and we needed to have her okay.

CHAPTER 19

Ferlisha

I suspected that they were talking between themselves without using words, but I was still surprised when they finally told me what it was that they were planning on doing. Their plan was dirtier than I thought it was going to be.

They were going to take my virginity and I wasn't going to know who was going to do that. They were going to put a blindfold on my head, it was going to cover my eyes, everything was going to be dark, and when one of them was inside of me, I would feel like I was in heaven.

I was a little nervous, but there was no denying that I was where I wanted to be.

Lester came in with the blindfold in his hands, asking me if I was okay with this. After all, I was going to have to trust them that they were going to do this the way they said it was going to happen. First, they were going to put the blindfold on me, and then they were going to penetrate me. And when that happened, I would feel like I was in heaven.

I nodded. It was the only thing I could do right now, anyway. He was happy with that and he even smiled, which was something that he was doing more often recently.

After putting the blindfold on me, I felt his finger moving between my lips, as if he was teasing me and as if to say that he was going to be fucking my mouth pretty soon. Just thinking about that, I couldn't wait until it was happening.

My heart was pounding like a jackhammer in my chest and it was the first time I was feeling so nervous. When I was a little younger than I was right now, I thought that losing my virginity was no big deal, but now I realized how wrong I was. My body was getting so much hotter by the second that I feared I wasn't going to last until this was over.

I heard Lester walking back to where he was and then I felt something, or rather someone, making the bed sag. I knew that it could only be one of the guys. He was going to take my virginity. It was all happening a little too fast, though.

I thought that they were going to take their time and compete among themselves to figure out who should first take my virginity, but it seemed that they didn't want to do that.

They were taking their time, but this was still happening a little too fast. I was enjoying every moment of it, and I still wished it would never end.

I felt his hands on my legs and then he widened their gap. I then felt his hands moving around my legs and pulling me slightly to him.

I wondered who he was, if he was the same one that was also my fiancé from back when I was going to get married, but the thought didn't stay in my mind for more than a couple of seconds before fading away. It didn't matter right now.

He didn't say anything, because of course he wasn't going to. He wasn't going to reveal his identity to me all of a sudden and ruin their little secret. I was okay with that, as I was supposed to be.

I felt his lips kissing my legs, his fingers moving over the skin, applying the right amount of pressure and massaging the skin the only way he could. I still didn't know who he was, and I had no idea who he might be. All I knew was that I was enjoying every moment of what was happening right now.

When he was done kissing and loving my legs, he pulled me even closer to him and I felt that he was going to finally penetrate me.

My pussy was quivering and was getting hot as time passed, and I had no idea why I was getting so desperate. It was a good thing that I felt that now this was happening slowly. The longer our sex took, the better it was for me.

I arched my back slightly when I felt his finger moving against my clit. He was just circling on it, sometimes rubbing it, and other times pressing against it. He knew how and when to hit all the right spots. He was relentless, and every time that I felt his finger scratching against my clit, I felt like I was going to come. And I wouldn't be just coming, but also spasming and I was pretty sure I would feel like I was going to pass out.

I just wished that he could say something so that I could know who he was, but then that would defeat the whole purpose of this, wouldn't it? I asked myself, and it wasn't really a question.

"Please, make this last as much as possible," I pleaded and I didn't know if they even heard me. I felt like I didn't hear anything coming out of my mouth, and that was saying something, considering that everyone always said that my voice was loud.

He moved his hands around my thighs and then grabbed them, pulling me a little more slightly to him again. I then felt his cock pressing against my pussy and that he was finally ready to penetrate me. Sweat was covering my body and I was feeling quite wet thanks to it.

And yet, I didn't even think about slowing things down even more than they already were. Just like I said before, the guys were taking their time and when this man was inside of me, I would change my mind about it. I would feel that this was happening way too fast.

I felt his fingers digging slightly into my skin and that was almost enough to make me go over the edge. I tried to shoot my hand to where my clit was and I was going to start rubbing it. And I was on the verge of doing it when his hand grabbed mine all of a sudden, stopping it.

"Why?" I asked, my body begging for release. One of the things I noticed that was happening right now was the fact that he was almost torturing me. He was holding me in place, not much was happening, and yet everything was happening at the same time.

It was like I was frozen in time. I was even beginning to feel that I was having difficulty breathing, which was something I never thought would happen in my life. I never thought I would be feeling so much anxiety.

He didn't respond, just like I thought he wasn't going to. I couldn't even know if his hand was slightly more callous or soft, like Lester's. I tried to find out, but it was pointless.

He was holding me with just his hands, his fingers were slightly digging into my skin, and he was breathing slowly. He was milking this moment so much that I thought it would never end.

I couldn't even start exciting my clit so that I could finally have an orgasm right now. The man that was doing me was relentless and cruel and I expected nothing different.

I then felt his dickhead nudging against the entrance of my little snatch, and I knew that meant things were finally going to go to the next level. He was going to penetrate me, and then he would pop my hymen, and then he would go all the way down to my cervix. When he was there, I would feel so much pain and pleasure at the same time, and yet I would still want things to keep on going.

I felt him taking a long breath and then he thrust his hips slightly, breaching the initial barrier. I then felt his dick as it kept on sliding farther inside of me, and then he stopped when he encountered one more barrier. I knew that he found my hymen and that now he was going to pop it. The only problem with that was that he was just taking so long and that was only making me feel more anxious. My heart was so tight I thought it was going to stop beating.

I was still trying to figure out who exactly was taking my virginity, but also that to keep doing so was pointless. Entirely so.

With another thrust of his hips, he popped my hymen and I arched my toes. Sweat was all over my body, covering it, and I felt so much pain I thought I was going to pass out.

The only thing that was keeping me here in this reality was his dick, and it wasn't stopping where he popped my hymen. If anything, he kept on doing what he was doing and then, when I felt that all of his inches were inside of me, he gave me a sign that it wasn't what was happening. He was only halfway inside of me.

And that was more frightening than I thought it was going to be.

As usual, he didn't say anything, but then he started to roll his hips as he began to fuck me. He was doing it slowly from the beginning, most likely realizing that I was feeling too much pain. I could feel pain all over my body and it was almost destroying me from the inside out. The only thing that was holding me in this reality was his dick inside of me, and that was mesmerizing.

It was bliss and I was never going to forget it.

I could feel my breathing quickening as he let go of my hand and I could finally do what I wanted to do, looking to make our sex even more exciting and pleasing. I started to rub my clit over and over, my pace frenetic from the get-go. I was just happy that he was allowing me to do that, given what happened before. I thought that he was going to grab my hand again.

And in no moment at all, I was coming all over his dick and it was the most delicious and exciting thing that ever happened in my life. Finally, I was complete. I just lost my V-card and it was something that was always going to remain in my mind.

I knew that he was free of STDs and that I was going to take all the needed precautions when it came to pregnancy, so he was fucking me without protection and he could come inside of me and I knew I wouldn't get pregnant.

This couldn't be happening any other way, too.

I could feel him erupting inside of me a moment later, and it was just magical. So much so that my breathing was returning to normal. Now that we were already at this point in our sex, I was getting used to it and so was the man that had just taken my virginity.

I could feel his rod throbbing and spasming inside of me, and I made sure that I kept my tunnel clenched around it so that it didn't slip out. And, it didn't. He remained inside of me even after his prick stopped throbbing and shooting out his come.

I kind of wished he got me pregnant, but it was something that we would have to discuss later. Right now, I was just happy that I wasn't a virgin anymore.

And when I thought that they were finally going to take off the blindfold, the guy that was fucking me moved away and then climbed off the bed, making space for his replacement. The latter was soon on top of me and then he grabbed me, dragging me toward him.

And then, it happened a little too fast, but he fucked me until he was blowing his jizz in there, where the first guy ate me, and I knew that he was happy with that. So much so that he pulled out without saying anything or complaining. He was just so happy that he was part of this, that he was finishing taking my virginity too.

My body was all sweaty and I knew that things were far from over.

I knew that so much that I wasn't surprised when the third and last guy grabbed me, dragging me toward him and then impaling me until his dick was all the way in, going as far as touching my cervix.

It was still as painful as before, but also so much better. The guy was relentless from the get-go and when he was pumping out his milk in my waiting, begging sex, he was more jubilant than I thought a man could ever be.

After he pulled out and my body fell on the bed, I knew that so much more was going to happen, that it was going to be painful, but also that I had a victorious smile on my face and that I couldn't wait for round two.

FERLISHA'S EPILOGUE

So, who was my fiancé before all this happened? I asked myself, but I knew the answer already. I didn't even know why I kept on making that question to myself even after I found out the answer a long time ago and decided not to say anything about it. The guys weren't jubilant about it, but they couldn't do anything.

When it came to my happiness, it was the most important thing for them.

The sun was high in the sky, bright, and warm when I came back to the mansion where we had been locked up. It was imposing and just as big as before, and part of me didn't want to let me go in there. But I felt that it needed to be done, and that I couldn't be doing this with anyone accompanying me.

I felt that I was finally going to find out what happened.

My heart was a little tight, but I went on. I opened the door of the mansion, noticing that the signs that the police had been in this place weren't here anymore. They checked everything they could, found some cameras, but that no signal, of any form, came out of this place during the time when we were here.

When they said that to me, I was puzzled about it, but now it was beginning to make sense.

I did some digging and I found out that Iov, Danilo, and Lester already knew me before the wedding. I didn't tell them anything about that, and I knew that I didn't have to.

After all, they already suspected that they already knew me, even though what they knew about me was nothing more than a memory they could never recover.

And they were okay with that. They were okay with it because they wanted to start things over, which was happening right now. They were happy that they could finally start to move away from what their lives were like, especially when it came to Iov's life.

He didn't want to continue being an assassin, even though it was difficult for him to tell the Walter Group that it was his choice. Danilo and Lester were helping him with that, and I knew that they were going to come up with something. They were going to find a solution, but it was going to take some time until that happened.

For the time being, I was focused on what I was doing. I found myself in the main hall, where everything started to happen between us. It was where I met Iov, Danilo, and then Lester, in that order. The memories that this place brought back were forever going to remain in my mind, and I was okay with that.

After forgetting so much about my life, it was high time I started remembering some things, and one of them was who could have thought that locking us in this place was something that he or she should do.

She…

I had a sudden realization that left me gasping for air. I never thought that the solution was so obvious. I even felt that my heart was going to stop beating, which made me support my hand against the wall that was by my side.

I looked up, ending my smile when I realized that I was… The culprit behind everything. I was the one who set us up, who locked us in this mansion, and it just made sense. Danilo, Iov, and Lester wanted me and they were going to kill each other if I didn't do something about it.

It was for that reason that I decided to give ourselves a special drink that made us forget who we were to each other. It was a little dangerous, especially for our health, but I still decided to do it.

I was also a little conflicted about my feelings for them, my parents always saying that I was supposed to choose just one, and when I chose one of them, I feared that I was making a big mistake. But not in the way that I was choosing the wrong guy, but that I wanted all of them at the same time.

I just had too much love in my heart for those men, and things couldn't be any better right now. I was with those men, they were in love with me, and we were all living together under the same roof.

I was the one who set us up, drugged us, and it happened while we were already in this mansion, right after the wedding. This was a special place for us, where we always came when we needed privacy. We had a long, heated discussion about what we should do, and it was then that I proposed that we should get a drink.

And that drink was drugged with the 'medicine' that I put in it.

I knew that I could never forgive myself for what I did, but now it was pointless to bring it up. I knew that coming back to the mansion was going to give me what I was looking for and I was happy with the answer I got, even though I wanted to forget it again. Just like when I found out who my fiancé or husband was. Semantics… That was nothing more than it was and I would do well to keep that in mind.

I shook my head, repositioned myself so that I was standing up straight in the main hall, and then I looked over my shoulder one more time. It was the last time that I was in this mansion and I was happy with that. I wanted to never come here again and I was pretty sure that the guys would be thinking the same thing, if they found out that I was here.

This mansion was always going to bring back memories to me, and that was okay. I just wanted to continue from where our lives restarted.

IOV'S EPILOGUE

Telling the Walter Group that I didn't want to work for them anymore was never going to be easy, and thus I wasn't surprised when we had to kill one of our guards. He was from the Walter Group and had come here to kill me.

They now considered me a traitor, and that was never going to change. The good thing was that, thanks to Danilo and Lester's influence in the world of politics, I should be safe, or as much as I could be.

It was going to be difficult, but I had someone special by my side that was always giving me all the support I needed. I had her with my right arm over her shoulders, and she was watching TV with me without saying anything. Danilo and Lester were away, out doing something or working, and in the meantime, I worked from home, selling tips for the right people on the dark web.

I knew that it was risky, but we needed the money. Maintaining our safety was difficult and pricey.

She was my emotional support.

She craned her head so that she was looking at me, blinking once and slowly. She was studying my face to see if she could figure out what it was that I was thinking, but that was difficult. Ferlisha always said that I was beginning to smile more often, but that wasn't entirely true. Even though I was starting to lead a happier life with her, I was always fearing for my life.

"This show's a little boring," she said, purring against my chest and I knew that she was looking only for one thing. She wanted my cock and it was hard and just waiting for her to do whatever she wanted. She could put her hand under my shorts and I wouldn't do anything about it. I wouldn't stop her.

After she lost her virginity on that special afternoon that would always remain in my mind, she started to gain more confidence when it came to pleasing us.

It was as if she was managing to read my mind this time. The show was indeed boring and thus she was looking to do something different. Something more exciting, that was going to make her heart beat faster, and I was more than willing to give her that.

"Do you want to do it?" I murmured into her ear, nibbling on her earlobe and I knew that she said yes when she nodded. It was everything I needed to see from her, and thus I helped her with lowering my shorts and underwear. When my cock came springing out, looking confident and mean, she was already with her small hand around it.

"I want to do much more than that," she replied and I knew that she was telling the truth. So much so that I wasn't surprised when she was already applying her perfect technique as she slid the skin of my prick up and down, applying a little bit more pressure on my mushroom-like dickhead.

She was going to make me come and there was no denying that it was her plan.

We were in one of the living rooms in the mansion and anyone could be watching us doing this. Anyone, and yet knowing that was only making me feel even more lust than normal.

I shut my eyes and let Ferlisha keep moving her hand up and down, hardening my prick even more than it already was.

It was like my mind was blocking everything that was around me. My balls were getting tenser and hotter all of a sudden, and I just knew that, when she wrapped her lips around my dickhead, I would come. I would come all over the inside of her mouth and it would be a moment I would never forget.

"Fuck, you are always so good at this," I murmured, parting my lips when she wrapped her tiny mouth around my prick and started to give me a blowjob. She was going up and down on my man tool, and I couldn't help but already explode inside her mouth when it happened.

I could feel my prick throbbing and spasming inside it, and another good thing about it was that she wasn't even surprised. She was taking everything that I was pumping inside her mouth, and I knew she was finding it delicious. So much so that when I reopened my eyes and she looked up, I noticed that her lips were coated with my come. I knew that if it was up to her, she would be continuing the blowjob for as long as possible, but that wasn't an option right now.

I knew that because I had another client calling me on my phone and even though Ferlisha was the most important woman in my life, I needed to pick it up. And I did that, much to her disappointment.

She pulled her head back up and looked at my eyes again. When I was going to say 'hi' to the person that was calling me, she wrapped her hand around my gland one more time, giving it a little squeeze.

I knew that there was some time until my friend had to tell me what he had to say, and thus Ferlisha had all the time in the world.

"Thought you could escape me so easily?" She asked, and I knew that it wasn't a real question. In fact, she was only looking for the reaction that showed up on my face. She smiled, seeing how surprised I was. When it came to being filthy and dirty, Ferlisha was a professional at it.

I knew that my blowjob was far from over and that it was going to make the other guys a little jealous of me.

DANILO'S EPILOGUE

I was with my men and I still felt like I was alone. One of the reasons for that was because I was missing my muse and I knew she was looking for me. I was somewhere in the city, trying to find out what she was hiding from me. Even though I knew I was in the right, I just wanted to know if she was my true wife – from back when she got married.

I knew that if she found out what I was doing, she would be hurt, but that was why I was doing this without her knowledge. I was also aware that this could hurt my relationship with her beyond repair, but I was still going along with it. The problem was that when I had something nagging in my mind, I just couldn't brush it off.

"Boss, I don't think you should be doing this." It was my second-in-command saying that and even though I knew he was only looking out for me, it was still difficult for me to even consider what he was saying. I wasn't going to take it into consideration because it already took me so long until I made up my mind about this.

I missed the touch of her lips against mine and I knew that she was thinking the same thing, even at this moment when she should be working or reading in our house, but it was just the way she was. When Ferlisha had her mind set on something, she always completed her goal, just like me.

Just thinking that already brought a smile to my face. I could even almost hear her voice speaking to me right now, showing me just how much I missed her.

I took a deep breath in, ran my hand over my face, and opened the door of the room. It was located in a building somewhere in town, where she last lived before meeting Iov for the first time.

He was the first one that she started to befriend, and then she fell in love with him, and then I and Lester showed up in her life, confusing her mind more than it already was.

I had to take another deep breath. It was the first time I was feeling so nervous, which was something that surprised my men. They were looking at me a little flabbergasted about what was going on right now.

They wished they could do something about it that was more than what they were doing, but right now the only thing that they could continue doing was helping me.

I stepped inside the room and then I walked over to her old diary. It was on top of a desk on the other side of the room and waiting for me. I knew that her diary contained everything I needed to know, everything that happened in our past when she was no more than 18 years old.

It was around that age when she first met Iov and that was when their life turned upside down. She found out that he worked for the Walter Group, that he was an assassin, and she couldn't brush it off.

I picked up her diary and when I was going to open it, my hand was shaking so much I just couldn't finish what I was doing. I thought I was stronger than this. After all, I spent so much time making my mind up about it, and now I was going to chicken out on it? I didn't know, but my hand was shaking so much that I had to put down the diary.

It was almost like I could see her standing right in front of me and saying that she couldn't believe what I was doing, that I was destroying the relationship of trust that she established between us.

My second-in-command was right. I shouldn't be doing this. I should be respecting my lover's wish. If I found out who her initial husband was, everything about us would change.

I would never be able to look at her with the same eyes and if she found out that I knew about it, which she most likely would, then she would also never be able to forgive me.

I heard my second-in-command coming over, smiling softly.

"I knew that you were going to change your mind about it. That's why we need to do something about this diary so that it's never brought up again."

My second-in-command knew so much about my life it was mind-boggling. I trusted him so much and it only made sense that he was the person he was to me. My second-in-command, my best friend, and pretty much everything else.

"You're right. Let's burn this diary so that nobody else can find out the truth. It's like you said. Even though I'm utterly curious about it, it's unimportant and it won't make me feel any different, not in a good way, at least."

He smiled again and then fished out of his pocket his lighter. He gave it to me and then I burned the diary with it, dropping it back on the floor. I watched as the flames consumed it, and I was feeling happy. More content than normal now that I was making this choice.

I knew that I'd promised Ferlisha that I wouldn't look for the truth, and as far as I was concerned, even though I began to betray her trust, in the end I didn't go through with it.

My mind was set and my life wasn't going to change much more than it already was. I was always going to be the don of my family, I was always going to be dangerous, and I was always also going to be under the crosshairs of the government and pretty much everyone else that wanted to kill me.

All in all, even though I was married and my life was much better for it, the professional side of it wasn't going to change more than it already was.

I shook my head and reopened my eyes. It was better to focus on Ferlisha and to keep on making her happy. Also, I was content that things were going well between me, Iov, and Lester.

They were beginning to become my friends as well.

LESTER'S EPILOGUE

Oh boy, this couldn't be happening any differently, I thought, ripping the dress off her body and checking out the perfection that it was, and all her curves and pretty much everything that made her the person she was. There was a point when I feared I would never find love in my life, especially after the failed attempts that happened with other women, but things were different now.

And it was also something that was a little bit more curious. Something that could leave anyone flabbergasted. We were doing this back in that old mansion. We were still looking for the person that locked us up in here and we would never give up on finishing that, but our searches were lessening in terms of intensity. It wasn't that we weren't losing interest in it, but that our lives were more focused on something else at the moment.

And that was none other than pleasing Ferlisha as much as needed.

She looked so exposed in front of us, and we were around her. We surrounded her and now she had no other place where she could go. Ferlisha had been running everywhere in the mansion and now she trapped herself here. It was more like that we led her here, but that was just a detail.

The important thing was that she was naked, from top to bottom, and that her body was the same as when we first met.

She was so stunning that my dick was already getting hard and all I could think about was how much I wanted to be pounding in and out of her ass. Ferlisha was thinking the same thing too, which was why she couldn't erase the smile on her face.

"Are you sure that you want to do this?" I asked, approaching her and then putting myself behind her. I started to massage her shoulders and she was loving what I was doing. So much so that she turned her head so that we could kiss and it happened easily.

When we broke the kiss, she said, "Of course. I've always been waiting for this, and I know you think the same way."

There was no point in saying anything else about it, and we all knew that we wanted one thing. Coming inside her soiled, warm pussy. And it was with that thought in mind that I pushed her down so that she was on all fours on the floor, her ass raised and pointed to us. We could do so many things with it, and yet we were going to do only one.

My hand was curled around my cock and I was already stroking it gently. It was already hard and it didn't need any more reason to continue being hard than it already was, but I just loved the feeling of my hand on my dick. I was pretty sure that the guys thought the same way, I remembered with some amusement on my face.

Her ass was just so round, big, and succulent. It was hard for me to focus on what was going around me, and I was thus focusing only on what was happening right in front of my eyes.

She wiggled her ass, just waiting for me to go in there and slide my prick between her ass. Given the way Ferlisha kept on wiggling her butt, I was pretty sure that it was the only thing in her mind right now, and I loved that about her.

"Fuck, she's always so hot," Danilo muttered and it was an understatement. So much so that I smiled and he didn't say anything about it. He was always a little busy when he thought that someone was mocking him. Talk about not having enough confidence, I thought.

I couldn't deny that there was still some competition between us, but this time it was more on the healthy side. There was always going to be some of that among us, and that was okay.

I grabbed her ass, widening it slightly and then sliding my prick between her asscheeks and into her waiting pussy. I knew that she was begging for it, and I was giving her exactly that. This time, it was much easier to be inside of her than it was the first time this happened, and I could feel her body shuddering and quivering in response. It was almost too much for Ferlisha, and it was taking her everything she had not to pass out.

I shifted so that I was even further inside of her. We were doing this without protection and it was the only way that this could be happening. When it came to Ferlisha, she just wouldn't have it any other way. She wanted skin on skin, and I was giving her exactly that.

"How are you feeling right now?" I asked, moving my hand around her waist and feeling it. I massaged it sometimes, giving her exactly what she wanted. I could feel her body trembling slightly, and I knew that she was about to come. She would come so hard it would be marvelous. Maybe we could even record it, though we would only do that with her permission.

"Much better than ever before in my life," she muttered and I had no idea if, this time, she was going to take her pregnancy prevention pills or not. I supposed that it didn't matter.

We wanted to get her pregnant. We had been thinking about doing it recently, and we knew that she was begging for it. Ferlisha was much more mature this time and she knew what she wanted. She wanted to grow old with us, and maybe I was going to make that happen.

"It's good to hear that," I said, moving my hand over her neck and feeling how rigid and warm it was. It couldn't be any different. When I started to roll my hips, it was like her body was moving as if it was part of mine, and I was loving it.

My prick was hard, my balls were tight, and I knew that I wasn't going to last much longer. I knew that, when I was erupting inside of her, everything was going to be so much better.

And when the time was right, when she was pregnant, I would be the one to choose the name of the baby. It was a promise that I was making to myself, and no one was going to stand in my way.

I heard one of the guys stepping over and standing in front of her. We were doing this in my old room in this mansion, and the fact that this was happening here and not somewhere else was telling, or at least it was looking like it was showing me that everything was going according to plan.

This was about me. Even though Ferlisha refused to tell me anything about it, I was pretty sure that I was her original husband. The first one. I was happy with sharing her with the other guys, but there was no denying that I was much more special to her. I knew that she knew what I was suspecting was the truth, and nothing was going to change that.

The only thing that was changing right now was the fact that I was already coming inside her soiled, wet pussy. It was like time was passing in slow motion for me, and I wouldn't be having this any other way. Even while I was still pumping my milk out inside of her, I was still pounding against her butt, the slapping sounds filling the room.

She was moaning so loudly it was just unbelievable. I thought she was going to pass out when she shut her eyes and didn't open them straight away, but then I noticed that it was nothing more than a baseless worry that sprouted up in my mind all of a sudden.

I could feel the last drops of my come filling her pussy. If there was a plaque to hang around her neck saying that she was our 'Cum Dump,' it would make this even more perfect than it was.

It was Danilo that was standing in front of her now, prying open her mouth and then sliding his prick inside it. He moved his hand over it and then cupped the back of it, easing his prick inside her mouth until he was ball-deep. Just seeing the developing situation before my eyes, I felt like I was losing this little competition that was developing between us, but then I realized that I was the one fucking her quivering snatch.

And she was loving every minute of it. If she were to get pregnant after this, I would be pretty sure I was the father.

And yet, I wasn't thinking about that right now. What I was thinking about was loving her mounds, especially now that it looked like I had to make some space for Iov. I liked him, but he was still dangerous and I knew that he would never change in that regard.

I started to love and worship her breasts with my mouth, spending as much time doing that as I was allowed to. I glided my hand over her belly for what felt like an eternity, rubbing her clit even while Iov rammed in and out of her sex. I was beginning to think that I should be the one doing that again, even though he was in his right to be where he was, claiming his spot inside of her.

And then, after he came inside of her, Danilo finished up with her mouth and came over so that he was behind her ample, round ass. He eased his prick in there, started ramming it in and out of her, and it wasn't long until they were coming together.

We were all sweaty and this was pretty sloppy, but when we were done, we were lying on the bed with happy smiles on our faces. We would never forget what happened here, and our lives felt complete.

The End

Looking for the first story in the series? It's this one:

1. Whose Baby Is It?: Reverse Harem BWWM Mafia Romance

Leave your review if you liked this novel. Thank you!

TEASER: WHOSE BABY IS IT?

Reverse Harem BWWM Mafia Romance

Orena

My heart was pounding, more so than it ever did in any other situation I was in before. I was waiting for them to come. Who were they going to be? I didn't know, but I was waiting for them nonetheless. I had to admit that I was so nervous I thought I was going to be biting my own nails, but time was passing and I was already sweating less.

I looked at my watch on my wrist, wondering when they were going to come. When my 'friends' suggested that I should come to this blind date with three distinct men, I didn't think I was going to find myself at this rundown building. Not only was it the kind of place where I would never go unless someone pointed a gun at my head, it was also located on the outskirts of the city, where nobody dared come to.

I took a deep breath, finding pride in the reflection I saw in the mirror. It was my reflection, highlighting the curves of my body. I was seated on a single chair in the middle of the room. Scanning my surroundings, I noticed that it didn't have much in terms of furniture. Certainly not much more than a bed, the chair where

I was seated on, and a dresser. I didn't dare to open one of its drawers, fearing that a cockroach would come jumping out of it.

I knew that my fears weren't baseless. I'd seen a cockroach when I was climbing the stairs to the room.

The clerk at the front desk, a scrawny and short man who couldn't be more than 20 years old, had regarded me with judging eyes. For him, it was quite curious that a woman like me, who looked imperious and ready to take on the world, had come to this dump.

But enough was enough about that. I didn't want to feel narcissistic or that I had too high of an opinion about myself. That wasn't the case at all.

This was a different type of hotel, where privacy was always kept at a maximum. I didn't even know the name of the clerk, who didn't have a pin on his chest. To be honest with myself, the mere looks of the clerk disgusted me. When was the last time he took a shower?

The stench that was coming from him... It was something I was forever going to remember, and it didn't matter how hard I tried to erase it.

When I dreamed about my types of men, I dreamed of hunky, powerful white bosses claiming me, doing whatever they wanted to me, and finally taking my precious virginity. I knew that it was something that would eventually happen, especially now that I was in college, but it was difficult for me to wait, regardless. Actually, for me, it was a lot more than that.

Whenever I was with my 'friends' and they boasted about what their first times were like, I felt ashamed of myself. They always boasted about how much pleasure they brought to their pairs, and I craved doing the same. That was why I was so nervous right now, wringing my hands.

It didn't matter how hard I told myself that everything was going to be okay, I wasn't going to know that for sure unless the men I was waiting for were in the room with me.

Before arriving here, I took care of myself, combed my hair, sprayed perfume over my body, and made sure that I shaved my pussy. The last thing I wanted, when the time was right, was to disappoint my dates.

It's what this was. Nothing more than a one-night stand with three men who were more than willing to share me.

As for them, they were going to come, but it was going to take a while.

They were men used to doing whatever and everything they wanted to their partners. They knew they were commanding, influential studs who didn't wait before doing everything they could to stake their claim.

I stood up, beelining to the window, where I pushed up the segmented curtain, revealing what was outside. It was as if everything terrible that could happen outside was. Criminals, drug addicts, whores, and the like were outside, polluting the streets.

I wanted nothing more than to be far away from them. It was such a pity that the men that I matched with said that they were going to come, but that the place they had to go to had to be here. I tried, thanks to the privacy that the phone app provided me with, to convince them to go elsewhere, perhaps one of the luxurious hotels downtown, but they didn't budge.

I tried to tell them that I was uncomfortable coming here, but I gave up on that. The blind date was one of the most memorable events in my life. So much so that I was betting everything I had that I was going to lose my virginity here.

As if to show that my coming here wasn't a waste of time – and if it was, I would be disappointed that I had come all the way here for nothing – three cars pulled over by the building. Three men slid out of them, dressed in dark suits as if this was a business meeting.

That couldn't be the case. I was impressed by who they were or, at least, who they appeared to be. They looked so much like businessmen I wondered if my initial assumption was wrong. What if they were around here for something else? Perhaps they weren't even going to come up to the floor where I was, but I was clinging to hope nonetheless.

A moment later, when I perceived that they were coming toward the building, my heart started to race. It was as though I was going to have a heart attack. It was finally going to happen, wasn't it? I still struggled to come to terms that I had to put myself in this kind of situation.

I was going to have to lose my virginity to three men, and they were handsome and excessively sexy. My eyesight wasn't as good as it was when I was younger, but when I spotted them from afar, I knew that they were a sight for sore eyes. Sharp hair, flawless jawline, dark sunglasses, and beard still to be made.

The confidence with which they carried themselves was unmatched. I wondered again if I was going to disappoint them, but then I realized that it was too late to be fearing that. The three businessmen-looking 'partners' just stepped inside the building, and I knew that they were going to come for me.

A second later, I realized that they were chatting with the front desk clerk. I couldn't make out the words, but hearing their voices… I knew that they were different. They weren't just mundane, boring white men that had come to pop my cherry, but rather men from outside the country.

The thought that I was going to have my first time with foreigners was thrilling. Out of all my friends, none of them had sex with a foreigner and now I was going to do that with three of them.

I paced around in the room, wondering if this was some kind of mistake.

What if they were going to kidnap me? What if they were going to do unspeakable things to me and I could do nothing but scream for help over and over again? It was a possibility, but one I didn't want to entertain right now...

MORE BWWM DARK MAFIA AND OTHERS

SERIES ALPHA PREDATORS

1. Not my Wedding: A BWWM Dark Mafia Romance
2. Not my Vows: A BWWM Dark Mafia Romance
3. Not his Baby: A BWWM Dark Mafia Romance
4. Not my Fiancé: A BWWM Dark Mafia Romance
5. Not my Daughter: A BWWM Dark Mafia Romance

SERIES - PRETTY LIARS

1. Impossible to Choose: A BWWM Mafia Reverse Harem Romance
2. Kiss of Amnesia: Secret Baby BWWM Mafia Romance
3. Fake Boyfriend: Secret Baby BWWM Mafia Romance
4. A Baby for the Hitman: Secret Baby BWWM Mafia Romance
5. Mafia Boss's Surrogate: Amnesia BWWM Dark Mafia Romance

Other dark mafia romances:

Beg Me: An Arranged Marriage Dark Mafia Romance

Used by the Mafia Boss: A Dark Mafia Romance

Bait Me: A Dark Mafia Romance Bundle

Mafia Vassal: A Dark Italian Mafia Romance Bundle

Don't Cry: A Secret Baby Dark Mafia Romance

Seizing her Heart: A Bratva Mafia Romance Collection

Conquering my Queen: A Dark Mafia Romance Bundle

ABOUT THE AUTHOR

Ruthless mafiosos, gorgeous billionaires, and feisty heroines are just tiny fractions of Jolie Damman's stories. She breathes and lives dark romance, peppering each scene with intrigue and tension that sweep readers away.

A kiss isn't just that. When a characters' eyes meet another's, they speak of memories even they can't understand. It might hurt. There might be triggers, but it's all worth it in the end, and that's what Jolie Damman always believes.